SECOND CHANCE
WITH THE REBEL

SECOND CHANCE WITH THE REBEL

BY

CARA COLTER

First published in Great Britain 2013
by Mills & Boon, an imprint of Harlequin (UK) Limited.
Large Print edition 2013
Harlequin (UK) Limited, Eton House,
18-24 Paradise Road, Richmond, Surrey TW9 1SR

© Cara Colter 2013

ISBN: 978 0 263 23685 9

Harlequin (UK) policy is to use papers that are natural,
renewable and recyclable products and made from
wood grown in sustainable forests. The logging and
manufacturing process conform to the legal environmental
regulations of the country of origin.

Printed and bound in Great Britain
by CPI Antony Rowe, Chippenham, Wiltshire

CHAPTER ONE

"HUDSON GROUP, HOW may I direct your call?"

"Macintyre Hudson, please."

Could silence be disapproving? Lucy Lindstrom asked herself. As in, you didn't just cold-call a multimillion-dollar company and ask to speak to their CEO?

"Mr. Hudson is not available right now. I'd be happy to take a message."

Lucy recognized the voice on the other end of the phone. It was that same uppity-accented receptionist who had taken her name and number thirteen times this week.

Mac was not going to talk to her unless he wanted to. And clearly, he did not want to. She had to fight with herself to stay on the line. It would have been so much easier just to hang up the phone. She reminded herself she had no choice. She had to change tack.

"It's an urgent family matter."

"He's not in his office. I'll have to see if he's in the building. And I'll have to tell him who is calling."

Lucy was certain she heard faint suspicion there, as if her voice was beginning to be recognized also, and was on the blocked-caller list.

"You could tell him it's Harriet Freda calling." She picked a fleck of lavender paint off her thumbnail.

"I'll take your number and have him call you back when I locate him."

"It's okay. I'll hold," Lucy said with as much firmness as she could muster.

As she waited, she looked down at the paper in her purple-paint-stained hand. It showed a neat list of names, all of them crossed off save for one.

The remaining name stood out as if it was written in neon tubing.

The boy who ruined my life.

Macintyre W. Hudson. A voice whispered from her past, *Everybody just calls me Mac.*

Just like that, seven years slipped away, and she could see him, Mac Hudson, the most handsome boy ever born, with those dark, laughing eyes, that crooked smile, the silky chocolate hair, too long, falling down over his brow.

Just like that, the shiver ran up and down her spine, and Lucy remembered exactly why that boy had ruined her life.

Only, now he wasn't a boy any longer, but a man.

And she was a woman.

"Macintyre Hudson did not ruin your life," Lucy told herself sternly. "At best he stole a few moments of it."

But what moments those were, a voice inside her insisted.

"Rubbish," Lucy said firmly, but her confidence, not in great supply these days anyway, dwindled. It felt as if she had failed at everything she'd set her hand to, and failed spectacularly.

She had never gone to university as her parents had hoped, but had become a clerk in a bookstore in the neighboring city of Glen Oak, instead.

She had worked up to running her own store, Books and Beans, with her fiancé, but she had eagerly divested herself of the coffee shop and storefront part of the business after their humiliatingly public breakup.

Now, licking her wounds, she was back in her hometown of Lindstrom Beach in her old family home on the shores of Sunshine Lake.

The deeding of the house was charity, plain and simple. Her widowed mother had given it to Lucy before remarrying and moving to California. She said it had been in the Lindstrom family for generations and it needed to stay there.

And even though that was logical, and the timing couldn't have been more perfect, Lucy had the ugly feeling that what her mother really thought was that Lucy wouldn't make it without her help.

"But I have a dream," she reminded herself

firmly, shoring herself up with that before Mac came on the line.

Despite her failures, over the past year Lucy had developed a sense of purpose. And more important, she felt *needed* for the first time in a long time.

It bothered Lucy that she had to remind herself of that as she drummed her fingers and listened to the music on the other end of the phone.

The song, she realized when she caught herself humming along, was one about a rebel and had always been the song she had associated with Mac. It was about a boy who was willing to risk all but his heart.

That was Macintyre Hudson to a *T*, so who could imagine the former Lindstrom Beach renegade and unapologetic bad boy at the helm of a multimillion-dollar company that produced the amazingly popular Wild Side outdoor products?

Unexpectedly, the music stopped.

"Mama?"

Mac's voice was urgent and worried. It had

deepened, Lucy was sure, since the days of their youth, but it had that same gravelly, sensuous edge to it that had always sent tingles up and down her spine.

Now, when she most needed to be confident, was not the time to think of the picture of him on his website, the one that had dashed her hopes that maybe he had gotten heavy or lost all his hair in the years that had passed.

But think of it she did. No boring head-and-shoulders shot in a nice Brooks Brothers suit for the CEO of Hudson Group.

No, the caption stated the founder of the Wild Side line was demonstrating the company's new kayak, Wild Ride. He was on a raging wedge of white water that funneled between rocks. Through flecks of foam, frozen by the camera, Macintyre Hudson had been captured in all his considerable masculine glory.

He'd been wearing a life jacket, a Wild Side product that showed off the amazing broadness of his shoulders, the powerful muscle of sun-bronzed arms gleaming with water. More handsome than ever, obviously in his element, he'd had a look in his devil-dark eyes, a cast to his mouth and a set to his jaw that was one of fierce concentration and formidable determination.

Maybe he didn't have any hair. He'd been wearing a helmet in the photo.

"Mama?" he said again. "What's wrong? Why didn't you call on my private line?"

Lucy had steeled herself for this. Rehearsed it. In her mind she had controlled every facet of this conversation.

But she had not planned for the image that materialized out of her memory file, that superimposed itself above the image of him in the kayak.

A younger Mac Hudson pausing as he lifted himself out of the lake onto the dock, his body sun-browned and perfect, water sluicing off the rippling smooth lines of his muscles, looking up at her, with laughter tilting the edges of his ultra-sexy eyes.

Do you love me, Lucy Lin?

Never *I love you* from him.

The memory hardened her resolve not to be in any way vulnerable to him. He was an extraordinarily handsome man, and he used his good looks in dastardly ways, as very handsome men were well-known to do.

On the other hand, her fiancé, James Kennedy, had been homely and bookish and had still behaved in a completely dastardly manner.

All of which explained why romance played no part in her brand-new dreams for herself.

Fortified with that, Lucy ordered herself not to stammer. "No, I'm sorry, it isn't Mama Freda."

There was a long silence. In the background she could hear a lot of noise as if a raucous party was going on.

When Mac spoke, she took it as a positive sign. At least he hadn't hung up.

"Well, well," he said. "Little Lucy Lindstrom. I hope this is good. I'm standing here soaking wet."

"At work?" she said, surprised into curiosity.

"I was in the hot tub with my assistant, Celeste." His tone was dry. "What can I do for you?"

Don't pursue it, she begged herself, but she couldn't help it.

"You don't have a hot tub at work!"

"You're right, I don't. And no Celeste, either. What we have is a test tank for kayaks where we can simulate a white-water chute."

Lucy had peeked at their website on and off over the years.

The business had started appropriately enough, with Mac's line of outdoor gear. He was behind the name brand that outdoor enthusiasts coveted: Wild Side. First it had been his canoes. It had expanded quickly into kayaks and then accessories, and now, famously, into clothing.

All the reckless abandon of his youth channeled into huge success, and he was still having fun. Who tested kayaks at work?

But Mac had always been about having fun. Some things just didn't change.

Though he didn't sound very good-humored

right now. "I'm wet, and the kayak didn't test out very well, so this had better be good."

"This is important," she said.

"What I was doing was important, too." He sighed, the sigh edged with irritation. "Some things just don't change, do they? The pampered doctor's daughter, the head of student council, the captain of the cheerleading squad, used to having her own way."

That girl, dressed in her designer jeans, with hundred-dollar highlights glowing in her hair, looked at her from her past, a little sadly.

Mac's assessment was so unfair! For the past few years she had been anything but pampered. And now she was trying to turn the Books part of Books and Beans into an internet business while renting canoes off her dock.

She was painting her own house and living on macaroni and cheese. She hadn't bought a new outfit for over a year, socking away every extra nickel in the hope that she could make her dream a reality.

And that didn't even cover all the things she was running next door to Mama Freda's to do!

She would have protested except for the inescapable if annoying truth: she *had* told a small lie to get her own way.

"It was imperative that I speak to you," she said firmly.

"Hmmm. Imperative. That has a rather regal sound to it. A princess giving a royal command."

He was insisting on remembering who she had been before he'd ruined her life: a confident, popular honor student who had never known trouble and never done a single thing wrong. Or daring. Or adventurous.

The young Lucy Lindstrom's idea of a good time, pre-Mac, had been getting the perfect gown for prom, and spending lazy summer afternoons on the deck with her friends, painting each other's toenails pink. Her idea of a great evening had been sitting around a roaring bonfire, especially if a sing-along started.

Pre-Mac, the most exciting thing that had ever

happened to her was getting the acceptance let-
ter from the university of her choice.

"Pampered, yes," Mac went on. "Deceitful, no.
You are the last person I would have ever thought
would lower yourself to deceit."

But that's where he was dead wrong. He had
brought out the deceitful side in her before.

The day she had said goodbye to him.

Hurt and angry that he had not asked her to go
with him, to hide her sense of inconsolable loss,
she had tossed her head and said, "I could never
fall for a boy like you."

When the truth was she already had. She had
been so crazy in love with Mac that it had felt
as though the fire that burned within her would
melt her and everything around her until there
was nothing left of her world but a small, dark
smudge.

"I needed to talk to you," she said, stripping
any memory of that summer and those long,
heated days from her voice.

"Yes. You said. Imperative."

Apparently he had honed sarcasm to an art.

"I'm sorry I insinuated I was Mama Freda."

"Insinuated," he said silkily. "So much more palatable than lying."

"I had to get by the guard dog who answers your phone!"

"No, you didn't. I got your messages."

"Except the one about needing to speak to you personally?"

"Nothing to talk about." His voice was chilly. "I've got all the information you gave. A Mother's Day Gala in celebration of Mama Freda's lifetime of good work. A combination of her eightieth birthday and Mother's Day. Fund-raiser for all her good causes. She knows about the gala and the fund-raiser but has no idea it's honoring her. Under no circumstances is she to find out."

Lucy wondered if she should be pleased that he had obviously paid very close attention to the content of those messages.

Actually, the fund-raiser was for Lucy's good

cause, but Mama Freda was at the very heart of her dream.

At the worst point of her life, she had gone to Mama Freda, and those strong arms had folded around her.

"When your pain feels too great to bear, *liebling,* then you must stop thinking of yourself and think of another."

Mama had carried the dream with Lucy, encouraging her, keeping the fire going when it had flickered to a tiny ember and nearly gone out.

Now, wasn't it the loveliest of ironies that Mama was one of the ones who would benefit from her own advice?

"Second Sunday of May," he said, his tone bored, dismissive, "black-tie dinner at the Lindstrom Beach Yacht Club."

She heard disdain in his voice and guessed the reason. "Oh, so that's the sticking point. I've already had a hundred people confirm, and I'm expecting a few more to trickle in over the next week. It's the only place big enough to handle that kind of a crowd."

"I remember when I wasn't good enough to get a job busing tables there."

"Get real. You never applied for a job busing tables at the yacht club."

Even in his youth, Mac, in his secondhand jeans, one of a string of foster children who had found refuge at Mama's, had carried himself like a king, bristling with pride and an ingrained sense of himself. He took offense at the slightest provocation.

And then hid it behind that charming smile.

"After graduation you had a job with the town, digging ditches for the new sewer system."

"Not the most noble work, but honest," he said. "And real."

So, who are you to be telling me to get real? He didn't say it, but he could have.

Noble or not, she could remember the ridged edges of the sleek muscles, how she had loved to touch him, feel his wiry strength underneath her fingertips.

He mistook her silence for judgment. "It runs in my family. My dad was a ditchdigger, too. They had a nickname for him. Digger Dan."

She felt the shock of that. She had known Mac since he had come to live in the house next door. He was fourteen, a year older than she was. When their paths crossed, he had tormented and teased her, interpreting the fact she was always tongue-tied in his presence as an example of her family's snobbery, rather than seeing it for what it was.

Intrigue. Awe. Temptation. She had never met anyone like Mac. Not before or since. Ruggedly independent. Bold. Unfettered by convention. Fearless. She remembered seeing him glide by her house, only fourteen, solo in a canoe heavily laden with camping gear.

She would see his campfire burning bright against the night on the other side of the lake. It was called the wild side of the lake because it was undeveloped crown land, thickly forested.

Sometimes Mac would spend the whole week-end over there. Alone.

She couldn't even imagine that. Being alone over there with the bears.

The week she had won the spelling bee he had been kicked out of school for swearing.

She got a little Ford compact for her sixteenth birthday, while he bought an old convertible and stripped the engine in the driveway, then stood down her father when he complained. While she was painting her toenails, he was painstakingly building his own cedar-strip canoe in Mama's yard.

But never once, even in that summer when she had loved him, right after her own graduation from high school, had Mac revealed a single detail about his life before he had arrived in foster care in Lindstrom Beach.

Was it the fact that he had so obviously risen above those roots that made him reveal that his father had been nicknamed Digger Dan? Or had he changed?

She squashed that thing inside her that felt ridiculously and horribly like hope by saying, proudly, "I don't really care if you come to the gala or not."

She told herself she was becoming hardened to rejection. All the people who really mattered to Mama—except him—had said they would come. But her own mother had said she would be in Africa on safari at that time and many people from Lucy's "old" life, her high-school days, had not answered yet. Those who had, had answered no.

There was silence from Mac, and Lucy allowed herself pleasure that she had caught him off guard.

"And I am sorry about messing up *your* Mother's Day."

"What do you mean, *my* Mother's Day?" His voice was guarded.

That had always been the problem with Mac. The insurmountable flaw. He wouldn't let anyone touch the part of him that *felt*.

"I chose Mother's Day because it was symbolic. Even though Mama Freda has never been a biological mother, she has been a mother to so many. She epitomizes what motherhood is."

That was not the full truth. The full truth was that Lucy found Mother's Day to be unbearably painful. And she was following Mama Freda's own recipe for dealing with pain.

"I don't care what day you chose!"

"Yes, you do."

"It's all coming back now," he said sardonically. "Having a conversation with you is like crossing a minefield."

"You feel as if Mother's Day belongs to you and Mama Freda. And I've stolen it."

"That's an interesting theory," he said, a chill in his voice warning her to stop, but she wasn't going to. Lucy was getting to him and part of her liked it, because it had always been hard to get to Mac Hudson. It might seem as if you were, but then that devil-may-care grin materialized, saying *Gotcha, because I don't really care.*

"Every Mother's Day," she reminded him quietly, "you outdo yourself. A stretch limo picks her up. She flies somewhere to meet you. Last year Engelbert Humperdinck in concert in New York. She wore the corsage until it turned brown. She talked about it for days after. Where you took her. What you ate. Don't tell me it's not your day. And that you're not annoyed that I chose it."

"Whatever."

"Oh! I recognize that tone of voice! Even after all this time! Mr. Don't-Even-Think-You-Know-Me."

"You don't. I'll put a check in the mail for whatever cause she has taken up. I think you'll find it very generous."

"I'm sure Mama will be pleased by the check. She probably will hardly even notice your absence, since all the others are coming. Every single one. Mama Freda has fostered twenty-three kids over the years. Ross Chillington is clearing his filming schedule. Michael Boylston works in Thailand and he's coming. Reed Patterson is leaving football training camp in Florida to be here."

"All those wayward boys saved by Mama Freda." His voice was silky and unimpressed.

"She's made a difference in the world!"

"Lucy—"

She hated it that her name on his lips made her feel more frazzled, hated it that she could remember leaning toward him, quivering with wanting.

"I'm not interested in being part of Lindstrom Beach's version of a TV reality show. What are you planning after your black-tie dinner? No, wait. Let me guess. Each of Mama's foster children will stand up and give a testimonial about being redeemed by her love."

Ouch. That was a little too close to what she did have planned. Did he have to make it sound cheap and smarmy instead of uplifting and inspirational?

"Mac—"

"Nobody calls me Mac anymore," he said, a little harshly.

"What do they call you?" She couldn't imagine him being called anything else.

"Mr. Hudson," he said coolly.

She doubted that very much since, she could still hear a raucous partylike atmosphere unfolding behind him.

It occurred to her she would like to hang up on him. And she was going to, very shortly.

"Okay, then, Mr. Hudson," she snapped, "I've already told you I don't care if you don't come. I know it's way too much to ask of you to take a break from your important and busy schedule to honor the woman who took you in and pulled you back from the brink of disaster. Way too much."

Silence.

"Still, I know how deeply you care about her. I know it's you who has been paying some of her bills."

He sucked in his breath, annoyed that she knew that.

She pushed on. "Aside from your Mother's Day

tradition, I know you took her to Paris for her seventy-fifth birthday."

"Lucy, I'm dripping water on the floor and shivering, so if you could hurry this along."

She really had thought she could get through her life without seeing him again. It had been a blessing that he came back to Lindstrom Beach rarely, and when he had, she had been away.

Because how could she look at him without remembering? But then hadn't she discovered you could remember, regardless?

Once, a long, long time ago, she had tried, with a desperation so keen she could almost taste its bitterness on her tongue, to pry his secrets from him. Lying on the sand in the dark, the lake's night-blackened waters lapping quietly, the embers of their fire burning down, she had asked him to tell her how he had ended up in foster care at Mama Freda's.

"I killed a man," he whispered, and then into her shocked silence, he had laughed that laugh that was so charming and distracting and sensual, that laugh that hid everything he really was, and added, "With my bare hands."

And then he had tried to divert her with his kisses that burned hotter than the fire.

But he had been unable to give her the gift she needed most: his trust in her.

And that was the real reason she had told him she could never love a boy like him. Because, even in her youth, she had recognized that he held back something essential of himself from her, when she had held back nothing.

If he had chosen to think she was a snob looking down her nose at the likes of him, after all the time they had spent together that summer, then that was his problem.

Still, just thinking of those forbidden kisses of so many years ago sent an unwanted shiver down her spine. The truth was nobody wanted Mac to come back here less than she did.

"I didn't phone about Mama's party. I guess I thought I would tell you this when you came. But since you're not going to—"

"Tell me what?"

She had to keep on track, or she would be swamped by these memories.

"Mac—" she remembered, too late, he didn't want to be called that and plunged on "—something's wrong."

"What do you mean?"

"You knew Mama Freda lost her driver's license, didn't you?"

"No."

"She had a little accident in the winter. Nothing serious. She slid through a stop sign and took out Mary-Beth McQueen's fence and rose bed."

"Ha. I doubt if that was an accident. She aimed."

For a moment, something was shared between them. The rivalry between Mama and Mary-Beth when it came to roses was legendary. But the moment was a flicker, nothing more.

All business again, he said, "But you said it wasn't serious?"

"Nonetheless, she had to see a doctor and be retested. They revoked her license."

"I'll set her up an account at Ferdinand's Taxi."

"I don't mind driving her. I like it actually. My concern was that before the retesting I don't think she'd been to a doctor in twenty years."

"Thirty," he said. "She had her 'elixir.'"

Lucy was sure she heard him shudder. It was funny to think of him being petrified of a little homemade potion. The Mac of her memory had been devil-may-care and terrifyingly fearless. From the picture on his website, that much had not changed.

"I guess the elixir isn't working for her anymore," Lucy said carefully. "I drive her now. She's had three doctors' appointments in the last month."

"What's wrong?"

"According to her, nothing."

Silence. She understood the silence. He was wondering why Mama Freda hadn't told him about the driver's license, the doctor's appointments. He was guessing, correctly, that she would not want him to worry.

"It probably *is* nothing," he said, but his voice was uneasy.

"I told myself that, too. I don't want to believe she's eighty, either."

"There's something you aren't telling me."

Scary, that after all these years, and over the phone, he could do that. Read her. So, why hadn't he seen through her the only time it really mattered?

I could never fall for a boy like you.

Lucy hesitated, looked out the open doors to gather her composure. "I saw a funeral-planning kit on her kitchen table. When she noticed it was out, she shoved it in a drawer. I think she was hoping I hadn't seen it."

What she didn't tell him was that before Mama had shoved the kit away she had been looking out her window, her expression uncharacteristically pensive.

"Will my boy ever come home?" she had whispered.

All those children, and only one was truly her boy.

Lucy listened as Mac drew in a startled breath, and then he swore. Was it a terrible thing to love it when someone swore? But it made him the *old* Mac. And it meant she had penetrated his guard.

"That's part of what motivated me to plan the celebration to honor her. I want her to know—" She choked. "I want her to know how much she has meant to people before it's too late. I don't want to wait for a funeral to bring to light all the good things she's done and been."

The silence was long. And then he sighed.

"I'll be there as soon as I can."

"No! Wait—

But Mac was gone, leaving the deep buzz of the dial tone in Lucy's ear.

CHAPTER TWO

"WELL, THAT WENT well," Lucy muttered as she set down the phone.

Still, there was no denying a certain relief. She had been carrying the burden of worrying about Mama Freda's health alone, and now she shared it.

But with Mac? He'd always represented the loss of control, a visit to the wild side, and now it seemed nothing had changed.

If he had just come to the gala, Lucy could have maintained her sense of control. She had been watching Mama Freda like a hawk since the day she'd heard, *Will my boy ever come home?*

Aside from a nap in the afternoon, Mama seemed as energetic and alert as always. If Mama had received bad news on the health front,

Lucy's observations of her had convinced her that the prognosis was an illness of the slow-moving variety.

Not the variety that required Mac to drop everything and come now!

The Mother's Day celebration was still two weeks away. Two weeks would have given Lucy time.

"Time to what?" she asked herself sternly.

Brace herself. Prepare. Be ready for him. But she already knew the uncomfortable truth about Macintyre Hudson. There was no preparing for him. There was no getting ready. He was a force unto himself, and that force was like a tornado hitting.

Lucy looked around her world. A year back home, and she had a sense of things finally falling into place. She was taking the initial steps toward her dream.

On the dining-room table that she had not eaten at since her return, there were donated items that she was collecting for the silent auction at the Mother's Day Gala.

There were the mountains of paperwork it had taken to register as a charity. Also, there was a photocopy of the application she had just submitted for rezoning, so that she could have Caleb's House here, and share this beautiful, ridiculously large house on the lake with young women who needed its sanctuary.

One of her three cats snoozed in a beam of sunlight that painted the wooden floor in front of the old river-rock fireplace golden. A vase of tulips brought in from the yard, their heavy heads drooping gracefully on their slender stems, brightened the barn-plank coffee table. A book was open on its spine on the arm of her favorite chair.

There was not a hint of catastrophe in this well-ordered scene, but it hadn't just happened. You had to work on this kind of a life.

In fact, it seemed the scene reflected that she

had finally gotten through picking up the pieces from the last time.

And somehow, *last time* did not mean her ended engagement to James Kennedy.

No, when she thought of her world being blown apart, oddly it was not the front-page picture of her fiancé, James, running down the street in Glen Oak without a stitch on that was forefront in her mind. No, forefront was a boy leaving, seven years ago.

The next morning, out on her deck, nestled into a cushioned lounge chair, Lucy looked out over the lake and took a sip of her coffee. Despite the fact the sun was still burning off the early-morning chill, she was cozy in her pajamas under a wool plaid blanket.

The scent of her coffee mingled with the lovely, sugary smell of birch wood burning. The smoke curled out of Mama Freda's chimney and hung in a wispy swirl in the air above the water in front of Mama's cabin.

Birdsong mixed with the far-off drone of a plane.

What exactly did *I'll be there as soon as I can* mean?

"Relax," she ordered herself.

In a world like his, he wouldn't be able just to drop everything and come. It would be days before she had to face Macintyre Hudson. Maybe even a week. His website said his company had done 34 million dollars in business last year.

You didn't just walk away from that and hope it would run itself.

So she could focus on her life. She turned her attention from the lake, and looked at the swatch of sample paint she had put up on the side of the house.

She loved the pale lavender for the main color. She thought the subtle shade was playful and inviting, a color that she hoped would welcome and soothe the young girls and women who would someday come here when she had succeeded in transforming all this into Caleb's House.

Today she was going to commit to the color and order the paint. Well, maybe later today. She was aware of a little tingle of fear when she thought of actually buying the paint. It was a big house. It was natural to want not to make a mistake.

My mother would hate the color.

So maybe instead of buying paint today, she would fill a few book orders, and work on funding proposals for Caleb's House in anticipation of the rezoning. Several items had arrived for the silent auction that she could unpack. She would not give the arrival of Mac one more thought. Not one.

The drone of the plane pushed back into her awareness, too loud to ignore. She looked up and could see it, red and white, almost directly overhead, so close she could read the call numbers under the wings. It was obviously coming in for a landing on the lake.

Lucy watched it set down smoothly, turning the water, where it shot out from the pontoons, to silvery sprays of mercury. The sound of the engine cut from a roar to a purr as the plane glided over the glassy mirror-calm surface of the water.

Sunshine Lake, located in the rugged interior of British Columbia, had always been a haunt of the rich, and sometimes the famous. Lucy's father had taken delight in the fact that once, when he was a teenager, the queen had stayed here on one of her visits to Canada. For a while the premier of the province had had a summer house down the lake. Pierre LaPontz, the famous goalie for the Montreal Canadiens, had summered here with friends. Seeing the plane was not unusual.

It became unusual when it wheeled around and taxied back, directly toward her.

Even though she could not see the pilot for the glare of the morning sun on the windshield of the plane, Lucy knew, suddenly and without a shade of a doubt, that it was him.

Macintyre Hudson had landed. He had arrived in her world.

The conclusion was part logic and part instinct. And with it came another conclusion. That nothing, from here on in, would go as she expected it. The days when choosing a paint color was the scariest thing in her world were over.

Lucy had thought he might show up in a rare sports car. Or maybe on an expensive motorcycle. She had even considered the possibility that he might show up, chauffeured, in the white limo that had picked up Mama Freda last Mother's Day.

Take that, Dr. Lindstrom.

She watched the plane slide along the lake to the old dock in front of Mama Freda's. The engines cut and the plane drifted.

And then, for the first time in seven years, she saw him.

Macintyre Hudson slid out the door onto the pontoon, expertly threw a rope over one of the big anchor posts on the dock and pulled the plane in.

The fact he could pilot a plane made it more than evident he had come into himself. He was wearing mirrored aviator sunglasses, a leather jacket and knife-creased khakis. But it was the way he carried himself, a certain sureness of movement on the bobbing water, that radiated confidence and strength.

Something in her chest felt tight. Her heart was beating too fast.

"Not bald," she murmured as the sun caught on the luscious dark chocolate of his hair. It was a guilty pleasure, watching him from a distance, with him unaware of being watched. He had a powerful efficiency of motion as he dealt with mooring the plane.

He was broader than he had been, despite all the digging of ditches. All the slenderness of his youth was gone, replaced with a kind of mouth-watering solidness, the build of a mature man at the peak of his power.

He looked up suddenly and cast a look around, frowning slightly as if he was aware he was being watched.

Crack.

The sound was so loud in the still crispness of

the morning that Lucy started, slopped coffee on her pajamas. Thunder?

No. In horror Lucy watched as the ancient post of Mama Freda's dock, as thick as a telephone pole, snapped cleanly, as if it was a toothpick. As she looked on helplessly, Mac saw it coming and moved quickly.

He managed to save his head, but the falling post caught him across his shoulder and hurled him into the water. The post fell in after him.

A deathly silence settled over the lake.

Lucy was already up out of her chair when Mac's head reemerged from the water. His startled, furious curse shattered the quiet that had reasserted itself on the peaceful lakeside morning.

Lucy found his shout reassuring. At least he hadn't been knocked out by the post, or been overcome by the freezing temperatures of the water.

Blanket clutched to her, Lucy ran on bare feet across the lawns, then through the ancient ponderosa pines that surrounded Mama's house. She picked her way swiftly across the rotted decking of the dock.

Mac was hefting himself onto the pontoon of the plane. It was not drifting, thankfully, but bobbing cooperatively just a few feet from the dock.

"Mac!" Lucy dropped the blanket. "Throw me the rope!"

He scrambled to standing, found the rope and turned to look at her. Even though he had to be absolutely freezing, there was a long pause as they stood looking at one another.

The sunglasses were gone. Those dark, melted-chocolate eyes showed no surprise, just lingered on her, faintly appraising, as if he was taking inventory.

His gaze stayed on her long enough for her to think, *He hates my hair.* And *Oh, for God's sake, am I in my Winnie-the-Pooh pajamas?*

"Throw the damn rope!" she ordered him.

Then the thick coil of rope was flying toward her. The throw was going to be slightly short.

But if she leaned just a bit, and reached with all her might, she knew she could—

"No!" he cried. "Leave it."

But it was too late. Lucy had leaned out too far. She tried to correct, taking a hasty step backward, but her momentum was already too far forward. Her arms windmilled crazily in an attempt to keep her balance.

She felt her feet leave the dock, the rush of air on her skin, and then she plunged into the lake. And sank, the weight of the soaked flannel pajamas pulling her down. Nothing could have prepared her for the cold as the gray water closed over her head. It seized her; her whole body went taut with shock. The sensation was of burning, not freezing. Her limbs were paralyzed instantly.

In what seemed to be slow motion, her body finally bobbed back to the surface. She was in shock, too numb even to cry out. Somehow she floundered, her limbs heavy and nearly useless, to the dock. It was too early in the year for a ladder to be out, but since Mama no longer fostered kids she didn't put out a ladder—or maintain the dock—anyway.

Lucy managed to get her hands on the dock's planks, and tried to pull herself up. But there was a terrifying lack of strength in her arms. Her limbs felt as if they were made of Jell-O, all a-jiggle and not quite set.

"Hang on!"

Even her lips were numb. The effort it took to speak was tremendous.

"No! Don't." She forced the words out. They sounded weak. Her mind, in slow motion, rationalized there was no point in them both being in the water. His limbs would react to the cold water just as hers were doing. And he was farther out. In seconds, Mac would be helpless, floundering out beyond the dock.

She heard a mighty splash as Mac jumped back into the water. She tried to hang on, but she couldn't feel her fingers. She slipped back in, felt the water ooze over her head.

Lucy had been around water her entire life.

She had a Bronze Cross. She could have been a lifeguard at the Main Street Beach if her father had not thought it was a demeaning job. She had never been afraid of water.

Now, as she slipped below the surface, she didn't feel terrified, but oddly resigned. They were both going to die, a tragically romantic ending to their story—after all these years of separation, dying trying to save one another.

And then hands, strong, sure, were around her waist, lifting her. Her head broke water and she sputtered. She was unceremoniously shoved out of the water onto the rough boards of the dock.

Lucy dangled there, her elbows underneath her chest, her legs hanging, without the strength even to lift her head. His hand went to her bottom, and he gave her one more shove—really about as unromantic as it could get—and she lay on the dock, gasping, sobbing, coughing.

Mac's still in the water.

She squirmed around to look, but he didn't

need her. His hands found the dock and he pulled himself to safety.

They lay side by side, gasping. Slowly she became aware that his nose was inches from her nose.

She could see drops of water beaded on the sooty clumps of his sinfully thick lashes. His eyes were glorious: a brown so dark it melted into black. The line of his nose was perfect, and faint stubble, twinkling with water droplets, highlighted the sweep of his cheekbones, the jut of his jaw.

Her eyes moved to the sensuous curve of his lips, and she felt sleepy and drugged, the desire to touch them with her own pushing past her every defense.

"Why, little Lucy Lindstrom," he growled. "We have to stop meeting like this."

All those years ago it had been her capsized canoe that had brought them—just about the most unlikely of loves, the good girl and the bad boy—together.

A week after graduation, having won all kinds of awards and been voted Most Likely to Succeed by her class, she realized the excitement was suddenly over. All her plans were made; it was her last summer of "freedom," as everybody kept kiddingly saying.

Lucy had taken the canoe out alone, something she never did. But the truth was, in that gap of activity something yawned within her, empty. She had a sense of her own life getting away from her, as if she was falling in with other people's plans for her without really ever asking herself what *she* wanted.

A storm had blown up, and she had not seen the log hiding under the surface of the water until it was too late.

Mac had been over on the wild side, camping, and he had seen her get into trouble. He'd already been in his canoe fighting the rough water to get to her before she hit the log.

He had picked her out of the water, somehow not capsizing his own canoe in the process, and taken her to his campsite to a fire, to wait until the lake calmed down to return her to her world.

But somehow she had never quite returned to her world. Lucy had been ripe for what he offered, an escape from a life that had all been laid out for her in a predictable pattern that there, on the side of the lake with her rescuer, had seemed like a form of death.

In all her life, it seemed everyone—her parents, her friends—only saw in her what they wanted her to be. And that was something that filled a need in them.

And then Mac had come along. And effortlessly he had seen through all that to what was real. Or so it had seemed.

And the truth was, soaking wet, gasping for air on a rotting dock, lying beside Mac, Lucy felt now exactly as she had felt then.

As if her whole world shivered to life.

As if black and white became color.

It had to be near-death experiences that did that: sharpened awareness to a razor's edge. Because she was so aware of Mac. She could feel the warmth of the breath coming from his mouth in puffs. There was an aura of power around him that was palpable, and in her weakened state, re-assuring.

With a groan, he put his hands on either side of his chest and lifted himself to kneeling, and then quickly to standing.

He held out his hand to her, and she reached for it and he pulled her, his strength as easy as it was electrifying, to her feet.

Mac scooped the blanket from the dock where she had dropped it, shook it out, looped it around her shoulders and then his own, and then his arms went around her waist and he pulled her against the freezing length of him.

"Don't take this personally," he said. "It's a matter of survival, plain and simple."

"Thank you for clarifying," she said, with all the dignity her chattering teeth would allow. "You needn't have worried. I had no intention of ravishing you. You are about as sexy as a frozen salmon at the moment."

"Still getting in the last shot, aren't you?"

"When I can."

Cruelly, at that moment she realized a sliver of warmth radiated from him, and she pulled herself even closer to the rock-hard length of his body.

Their bodies, glued together by freezing, wet clothing, shook beneath the blanket. She pressed her cheek hard against his chest, and he loosed a hand and touched her soaking hair.

"You hate it," she said, her voice quaking.

"It wasn't my best entrance," he agreed.

"I meant my hair."

"I know you did," he said softly. "Hello, Lucy."

"Hello, Macintyre."

Standing here against Mac, so close she could feel the pebbles of cold rising on his chilled skin, she could also feel his innate strength. Warmth was returning to his body and seeping into hers.

The physical sensation of closeness, of sharing spreading heat, was making her vulnerable to other feelings, the very ones she had hoped to steel herself against.

It was not just weak. The weakness could be assigned to the numbing cold that had seeped into every part of her. Even her tongue felt heavy and numb.

It was not just that she never wanted to move again. That could be assigned to the fact that her limbs felt slow and clumsy and paralyzed.

No, it was something worse than being weak.

Something worse than being paralyzed.

In Macintyre Hudson's arms, soaked, her Winnie-the-Pooh pajamas providing as much protection against him as a wet paper towel, Lucy Lindstrom felt the worst weakness of all, the longing she had kept hidden from herself.

Not to be so alone.

Her trembling deepened, and a soblike sound escaped her.

"Are you okay?" he asked.

"Not really," she said as she admitted the full

truth to herself. It was not the cold making her weak. It was him.

Lucy felt a terrible wave of self-loathing. Was life just one endless loop, playing the same things over and over again?

She was cursed at love. She needed to accept that about herself, and devote her considerable energy and talent to causes that would help others, and, as a bonus, couldn't hurt her.

She pulled away from him, though it took all her strength, physical and mental. The blanket held her fast, so that mere inches separated them, but at least their bodies were no longer glued together.

History, she told herself sternly, was *not* repeating itself.

It was good he was here. She could face him, puncture any remaining illusions and get on with her wonderful life of doing good for others.

"Are you hurt?" he asked, putting her away from him, scanning her face.

She already missed the small warmth that had

begun to radiate from him. Again, she had to pit what remained of her physical and mental strength to resist the desire to collapse against him.

"I'm fine," she said tersely.

"You don't look fine."

"Well, I'm not hurt. Mortified."

His expression was one of pure exasperation. "Who nearly drowns and is mortified by it?"

Whew. There was no sense him knowing she was mortified because of her reaction to him. By her sudden onslaught of uncertainty.

They had both been in perilous danger, and she was worried about the impression her hair made? Worried that she looked like a drowned rat? Worried about what pajamas she had on?

It was starting all over again!

This crippling need. He had seen her once, when it seemed no one else could. Hadn't she longed for that ever since?

Had she pursued getting that message to him so incessantly because of Mama Freda? Or had it been for herself? To feel the way she had felt when his arms closed around her?

Trembling, trying to fight the part of her that wanted nothing more than to scoot back into his warmth, she reminded herself that feeling this way had nearly destroyed her. It had had far-reaching repercussions that had torn her family and her life asunder.

"This is all your fault," she said. Thankfully, he took her literally.

"I'm not responsible for your bad catch."

"It was a terrible throw!"

"Yes, it was. All the more reason you shouldn't have reached for the rope. I could have thrown it again."

"You shouldn't have jumped back in the water after me. You could have been overcome by the cold. I'm surprised you weren't. And then we both would have been in big trouble."

"You have up to ten minutes in water that cold before you succumb. Plus, I don't seem to feel cold water like other people. I white-water kayak.

I think it has desensitized me. But under no circumstances would I have stood on the pontoon of my plane and watched anyone drown."

Gee. He wasn't sensitive, and his rescue of her wasn't even personal. He would have done it for anyone.

"I wasn't going to drown," Lucy lied haughtily, since only moments ago she had been resigned to that very thing. He'd just said she had ten whole minutes. "I've lived on this lake my entire life."

"Oh!" He smacked himself on the forehead with his fist. "How could I forget that? Not only have you lived on the lake your entire life, but so did three generations of your family before you. Lindstroms don't drown. They die like they lived. Nice respectable deaths in the same beds that they were born in, in the same town they never took more than two steps away from."

"I lived in Glen Oak for six years," she said.

"Oh, Glen Oak. An hour away. Some consider Lindstrom Beach to be Glen Oak's summer suburb."

Lucy was aware of being furious with herself for the utter weakness of reacting to him. It felt much safer to transfer that fury to him.

He had walked away. Not just from this town. He had walked away from having to give anything of himself. How could he never have considered all the possibilities? They had played with fire all that summer.

She had gotten burned. And he had walked away.

And he had never even said he loved her. Not even once.

CHAPTER THREE

"YOU KNOW WHAT, Macintyre Hudson? You were a jerk back then, and you're still a jerk."

"May I remind you that you begged me to come back here?"

"I did not beg. I appealed to your conscience. And I personally did not care if you came back."

"You were a snotty, stuck-up brat and you still are. Here's a novel concept," Mac said, his voice threaded with annoyance, "why don't you try thanking me for my heroic rescue? For the second time in your life, by the way."

Because of what happened the first time, you idiot.

"If I needed a hero," she said with soft fury, "you are the last person I would pick."

That hit home. He actually flinched. And she was happy he flinched. *Snotty, stuck-up brat?*

Then a cool veil dropped over the angry sparks flickering in his eyes, and his mouth turned upward, that mocking smile that was his trademark, that said *You can't hurt me—don't even try.* He folded his arms over the deep strength of his broad chest, and not because he was cold, either.

"You know what? If I was looking for a damsel in distress, you wouldn't exactly be my first pick, either. You're still every bit the snooty doctor's daughter."

She felt all of it then. The abandonment. The fear she had shouldered alone in the months after he left. Her parents, who had always doted on her, looking at her with hurt and embarrassment, as if she could not have let them down more completely. The friends she had known since kindergarten not phoning anymore, looking the other way when they saw her.

She felt all of it.

And it felt as if every single bit of it was his fault.

"Just to set the record straight, maybe it's you who should be thanking me," she told him. "I came down here to rescue you. You were the one in the water."

"I didn't need your help…."

So, absolutely nothing had changed. She was, in his eyes, still the town rich girl, the doctor's snooty daughter, out of touch with what he considered to be real.

And he was still the one who didn't *need*.

"Or your botched rescue attempt."

The fury in her felt white-hot, as if it could obliterate what remained of the chill on her. Lucy wished she had felt *that* when she had seen him get knocked off the dock by the post. She wished, instead of running to him, worried about him, she had marched into her house and firmly shut the door on him.

She hadn't done that. But maybe it was never

too late to correct a mistake. She could do the right thing this time.

She stepped in close, shivered dramatically, letting him believe she was weak and not strong, that she needed his body heat back. Mac was wary, but not wary enough. He let her slip back in, close to him.

Lucy put both her hands on his chest, blinked up at him with her very best will-you-be-my-hero? look and then shoved him as hard as she could.

With a startled yelp, which Lucy found extremely satisfying, Macintyre Hudson lost his footing and stumbled off the dock, back into the water. She turned and walked away, annoyed that she was reassured by his vigorous cursing that he was just fine.

She glanced back. More than fine! Instead of getting out of the water, Mac shrugged out of his leather jacket and threw it onto the dock. Then, making the most of his ten minutes, he swam back to his plane.

Within moments he had the entire situation under control, which no doubt pleased him no end. He fastened the plane to the dock's other pillar, which held, then reached inside and tossed a single overnight bag onto the dock.

She certainly didn't want him to catch her watching. Why was she watching? It was just more evidence of the weakness he made her feel. What she needed to be doing was to be heading for a hot shower at top speed.

Lucy had crossed back into her yard when she heard Mama's shout.

"*Ach!* What is going on?"

She turned to see Mama Freda trundling toward her dock, hand over her brow, trying to see into the sun. Then Mama stopped, and a light came on in that ancient, wise face that seemed to steal the chill right out of Lucy.

"*Schatz?*"

Mac was standing on the dock, and had removed his soaking shirt and was wringing it out. That was an unfortunate sight for a girl trying to steel herself against him. His body was absolutely perfect, sleek and strong, water sluicing down the deepness of his chest to the defined ripples of his abs.

He dropped the soaked shirt beside his jacket and sprinted over the dock and across the lawn. He stopped at Mama Freda and grinned down at her, and this time his grin was so genuine it could have lit up the whole lake. Mama reached up and touched his cheek.

Then he picked up the rather large bulk of Mama Freda as if she were featherlight, and swung her around until she was squealing like a young girl.

"You're getting me all wet," she protested loudly, smacking the broadness of his shoulders with delight. "*Ach.* Put me down, galoot-head."

Finally he did, and she patted her hair into place, regarding him with such affection that Lucy felt something burn behind her eyes.

"Why are you all wet? You'll catch your death!"

"Your dock broke when I tried to tie to it."

"You should have told me you were coming," Mama said reproachfully.

"I wanted to surprise you."

"Surprise, schmize."

Lucy smiled, despite herself. One of Mama's goals in life seemed to be to create a rhyme, beginning with *sch,* for every word in the English language.

"You see what happens? You end up in the lake. If you'd just told me, I would have warned you to tie up to Lucy's dock."

"I don't think Lucy wants me tying up at her dock."

Only Lucy would pick up his dry double meaning on that. She could actually feel a bit of a blush moving heat into her frozen cheeks.

"Don't be silly. Lucy wouldn't mind."

He could have thrown her under the bus, because Mama would not have approved of anyone being pushed into the water at this time of year, no matter how pressing the circumstances.

But he didn't. Her gratitude that he hadn't

thrown her under the bus was short-lived as Mac left the topic of Lucy Lindstrom behind with annoying ease.

"Mama, I'm freezing. I hope you have *apfelstrudel* fresh from the oven."

"You have to tell me you're coming to get strudel fresh from the oven. That's not what you need, anyway. Mama knows what you need."

Lucy could hear the smile in his voice, and was aware again of Mama working her magic, both of them smiling just moments after all that fury.

"What do I need, Mama?"

"You need elixir."

He pretended terror, then dashed back to the dock and picked up his soaked clothing and the bag, tossed it over his naked shoulder. He returned and wrapped his arm around Mama's waist and let her lead him to the house.

Lucy turned back to her own house, her eyes still smarting from what had passed between those two. The love and devotion shimmered around them as bright as the strengthening morning sun.

That was why she had gone to such lengths to get Macintyre Hudson to come back here. And if another motive had lain hidden beneath that one, it had been exposed to her in those moments when his arms had wrapped around her and his heat had seeped into her.

Now that it was exposed, she could put it in a place where she could guard against it as if her life depended on it.

Which, Lucy told herself through the chattering of her teeth, it did.

Out of the corner of his eye, Mac saw Lucy pause and watch his reunion with Mama.

"Is that Lucy?" Mama said, catching the direction of his gaze.

"Yeah, as annoying as ever."

"She's a good girl," Mama said stubbornly.

"Everything she ever aspired to be, then."

Only, she wasn't a girl anymore, but a woman.

The *good* part he had no doubt about. That was what was expected of the doctor's daughter, after all.

Even given the circumstances he had noted the changes. Her hair was still blond, but it no longer fell, unrestrained by hair clips or elastic bands, to the slight swell of her breast.

Plastered to her head, it hadn't looked like much, but he was willing to bet that when it was dry it was ultrasophisticated, and would show off the hugeness of those dazzling green eyes, the pixie-perfection of her dainty features. Still, Mac was aware of fighting the part of him that missed how it used to be.

She had lost the faintly scrawny build of a long-distance runner, and filled out, a fact he could not help but notice when she had pressed the lusciousness of her freezing body into his.

She seemed uptight, though, and the level of her anger at him gave him pause.

Unbidden, he wondered if she ever slipped into the lake and skinny-dipped under the full moon.

Would she still think it was the most daring thing a person could do, and that she was risking arrest and public humiliation?

What made her laugh now? In high school it seemed as if she had been at the center of every circle, popular and carefree. That laugh, from deep within her, was so joyous and unchained the birds stopped singing to listen.

Mac snorted in annoyance with himself, reminding himself curtly that he had broken that particular spell a long time ago. Though if that was completely true, why the reluctance to return Lucy's calls? Why the aversion to coming back?

If that was completely true, why had he told Lucy Lindstrom, of all people, that his father had been a ditchdigger?

That had been bothering him since the words had come out of his mouth. Maybe that confession had even contributed to the fiasco on the dock.

* * *

"What's she doing?" Mama asked, worried. "Is she wet, too? She looks wet."

"We both ended up in the lake."

"But how?"

"A comedy of errors. Don't worry about it, Mama."

But Mama was determined to worry. "She should have come here. I would look after her. She could catch her death."

Mama Freda, still looking after everyone. Except maybe herself. She was looking toward Lucy's house as if she was thinking of going to get her.

He noticed the grass blended seamlessly together, almost as if the lawns of the two houses were one. That was new. Dr. Lindstrom had gone to great lengths to accentuate the boundaries of his yard, to lower any risk of association with the place next door.

Despite now sharing a lawn with its shabby

neighbor, the Lindstrom place still looked like something off a magazine spread.

A bank of French doors had been added to the back of the house. Beyond the redwood of the multilayered deck, a lawn, tender with new grass, ended at a sea of yellow and red tulips. The flowers cascaded down a gentle slope to the fine white sand of the private beach.

On the L-shaped section of the bleached gray wood of the dock a dozen canoes were upside down.

What was with all the canoes? He was pretty sure that Mama had said Lucy was by herself since she had come home a year ago.

A bird called, and Mac could smell the rich scent of sun heating the fallen needles of the ponderosa pine.

As he gazed out over the lake, he was surprised by how much he had missed this place. Not the town, which was exceptionally cliquey; you were either "in" or you were "out" in Lindstrom Beach.

Lucy's family had always been "in." Of course,

"in" was determined by the location of your house on the lake, the size of the lot, the house itself, what kind of boat you had and who your connections were. "In" was determined by your occupation, your membership in the church and the yacht club, and by your income, never mentioned outright, always insinuated.

He, on the other hand, had been "out," a kid of questionable background, in foster care, in Mama's house, the only remaining of the original cabins that had been built around the lake in the forties. Her house, little more than a fishing shack, had been the bane of the entire neighborhood.

And so the sharing of the lawn was new and unexpected.

"Do you and Lucy go in together to hire someone to look after the grounds?" he asked.

"No, Lucy does it."

That startled him. Lucy mowed the expansive lawns? He couldn't really imagine her pushing a lawn mower. He remembered her and her friends sitting on the deck in their bikinis while the "help" sweated under the hot sun keeping the grounds of her house immaculate. But he didn't want Lucy to crowd back into his thoughts.

"You look well, Mama," he said, an invitation for her to confide in him. He should have known it wouldn't be that easy.

"I look well. You look terrible." She gave his freezing, naked torso a hard pinch. "No meat on your bones. Eating in restaurants. I can tell by your coloring."

He thought his coloring might be off because he had just had a pretty good dunking in some freezing water, but he knew from long experience that there was no telling Mama.

They approached the back of her house. The porch door was choked with overgrown lilacs, drooping with heavy buds. Mac pushed aside some branches and opened the screen door. It squeaked outrageously. He could see the floorboards of her screened porch were as rotten as her dock.

He frowned at the attempt at a repair. Had she hired some haphazard handyman?

"Who did this?" he said, toeing the new board.

"Lucy," she said, eyeing the disastrous repair with pride. "Lucy helps me with lots of things around here."

His frown deepened. Somehow that was a Lucy he could never have imagined, nails between teeth, pounding in boards.

Though Mama had said nothing, he had suspected for some time the house was becoming too much for her, and this confirmed it.

"You should come to Toronto with me," he said. It was his opening move. In his bag he had brochures of Toronto's most upscale retirement home.

"Toronto, schmonto. No, you should move back here. That big city is no place for a boy like you."

"I'm not a boy anymore, Mama."

"You will always be my boy."

He regarded her warmly, searching her face for any sign of illness. She was unchanging. She had seemed old when he had first met her, and she really had never seemed to get any older. There was a sameness about her in a changing world that had been a touchstone.

Why hadn't she told him she had lost her license?

She was going to be eighty years old three days before Mother's Day. He held open the inside door for her, and they stepped through into her kitchen.

It, too, was showing signs of benign neglect: paint chipping from the cabinets, a door not closing properly, the old linoleum tiles beginning to curl. There was a towel tied tightly around a faucet, and he went and looked.

An attempted repair of a leak.

"Lucy's work?" he guessed.

"Yes."

Again, the Lucy he didn't know. "You just have to tell me these things," he said. "I would have paid for the plumber."

"You pay for enough already."

He turned to look at Mama, and without warning he was fourteen years old again, standing in this kitchen for the first time.

Harriet Freda's had been his fifth foster home in as many months, and despite the fact this one had a prime lakeshore location, from the outside the house seemed even smaller and dumpier and darker than all the other foster homes had been.

Maybe, he had thought, already cynical, they just sent you to worse and worse places.

The house would have seemed beyond humble in any setting, but surrounded by the magnificent lake houses, it was painfully shacklike and out of place on the shores of Sunshine Lake.

That morning, standing in a kitchen that cheerfully belied the outside of the house, Mac had been fourteen and terrified. That had been his first lesson since the death of his father: never let the terror show.

She had been introduced to him as Mama Freda, and she looked stocky and ancient. Her hair was a bluish-white color and frizzy with a bad perm. She had more wrinkles than a Shar-Pei. Mac thought she was way too old to be looking after other people's kids.

Still, she looked harmless enough, standing at her kitchen table in a frumpy dress that showed off her chunky build, thick arms and legs, ankles swollen above sensible shoes. She had been wearing a much-bleached apron, once white, aged to tea-dipped, and covered with faded blotches of berry and chocolate.

The niceties were over, the social worker was gone and he was standing there with a paper bag containing two T-shirts, one pair of jeans and a change of underwear. Mrs. Freda cast him a look, and there was an unmistakable friendly twinkle in deep-set blue eyes.

Well, there was no sense her thinking they were going to be on friendly terms.

"I killed a man," he said, and then added, "With my bare hands." He thought the *with my bare hands* part was a nice touch. It was actually a line from a song, but it warned people to stay back from him, that he was dangerous and tough.

And if Macintyre Hudson had wanted one thing at age fourteen, it was for people to stay back from him. He had been like a wounded animal, unwilling to trust again.

Mama Freda glanced up from what she was doing, stretching out an enormous piece of dough, thin and elastic, over the edges of her large, round kitchen table. She regarded him, and he noticed the twinkle was gone from her eyes, replaced with an immense sorrow.

"This is a terrible thing," she said, sinking into a chair. "To kill a man. I know. I had to do it once."

He stared at her, his mouth open. And when she beckoned to the chair beside hers, he abandoned his meager bag of belongings and went to it, as if drawn to her side by a magnet.

"It was near the end of the war," she said, looking at her hands. "I was thirteen. A soldier, he was—" she glanced at Mac, trying to decide how much to say "—hurting my sister. He had his back to me. I picked up a cast-iron pan and I crept up behind him and I hit him as hard as I could over his head. There was a terrible noise. Terrible. He fell off my sister. I think he was already dead, but I knew if he ever got up we were all doomed, and so I hit him again and again and again."

Mac had never heard silence like he heard in Mama Freda's kitchen right then. The clock ticking sounded explosive.

"So I know what this thing is," she said finally, "to kill a man. I know how you carry it within you. How you think of his face, and wonder who he was before the great evil overcame him. I wonder what his mother felt when he never came home, and if his sisters grieve him to this day, the way I grieve the brother who went to war and never came home."

Her hand crept out from under her apron and she laid it, palm up, on the table. An invitation. And Mac surprised himself by not being able to refuse that invitation. He put his hand on the table, too. Her hand closed around his, surprisingly strong for such an old lady.

"Look at me," she said.

And he did.

She did not say a word. She didn't have to. He looked deep into her eyes, and for the first time in a long, long time, he felt he was not alone.

That someone else knew what it was to suffer.

Later they ate the *apfelstrudel* she had finished rolling out on her kitchen table, and it felt as if his taste buds had come awake, as if he could taste for the first time in a long, long time, too, as if he had never tasted food quite so wondrous.

He started, in that moment, with warm strudel melting in his mouth, to do what he had sworn he would never do again. But he was careful never to call it that, and never to utter the words that would solidify it and make it real. For him, the admission of love was the holding of a samurai's sword that you would eventually plunge into your own heart.

But he had never altered the story he had told

her that day, not even when she had said to him once, "I know, *schatz,* there is nothing in you that could kill another person. Or anything. Not even a baby robin that fell from its nest. I have watched you carry bugs outside rather than swat them."

But he had never doubted that she really had killed that soldier, and she, too, carried bugs outside rather than swatting them.

Mama, with her enormous capacity to care for all things, had saved him.

And he owed it to her to be there for her if she needed him. It was evident from the state of her house that he hadn't been there in the ways she needed. And that Lucy, the one he had called the spoiled brat, had been. He felt the faintest shiver of something.

Guilt?

"Go shower," Mama said, and he drew himself back to the present with a shake of his head. "Nice and hot."

She was already reaching up high into her cabinet and Mac shuddered when the ancient brown bottle of elixir came down, and he hightailed it for the tiny bathroom at the top of the stairs.

When he came down, in dry clothes, she had a tumbler of the clear liquid poured.

"Drink. It will ward off the cold."

"I'm not cold."

"The cold you will get if you don't drink it!" She had that look on her face, her arms folded over her ample bosom.

There was no sense explaining to Mama you didn't get colds from being cold, that you got them from coming in contact with one of hundreds of viruses, none of which were very likely to be living in the freezing-cold water of Sunshine Lake.

He took the tumbler, plugged his nose and put it back. It burned to his belly and he felt his toes curl.

He set the glass down, and wiped his watering eyes. "For heaven's sakes, its schnapps!"

"Obstler," she said happily. "Not peppermint

sugar like they drink here. Ugh. Mine is made with apples. Herbs."

She was right, though—if there was any sneaky virus in him, no matter what the source, it would be gone now.

"Homemade, from my great-grandmother's recipe. Now, take some to Lucy. I have it ready." She passed him an unlabeled brown bottle of her secret elixir.

"I'm not taking it to Lucy." After that encounter on the dock, the less he had to do with Lucy the better.

He'd wanted to believe, after all this time, that Lucy, the girl who had not thought he was good enough, would have no power over him. He had seen the world. He'd succeeded. He'd expected Lucy and this town to be nothing more than a speck of dust from the past.

What he hadn't expected was the rush of feeling when he had seen her. Even dripping wet, near frozen, seeing Lucy on the dock calling to him, he had felt a pull so strong it felt as if his heart was coming from his chest. He'd been vulnerable, caught off guard, but still, there had always been something about her.

She still had that face, impish, unconventionally beautiful, that inspired warmth and trust, that took a man's guard right down, and left him in a place where he could be shoved into a lake by someone who weighed sixty pounds less than he did.

An old hurt surfaced, its edges knife-sharp.

I could never fall for a boy like you.

That was the problem with coming back to a place you had left behind, Mac thought. Old hurts didn't die. They waited. And those words, coming from Lucy, the one he had trusted with his ever-so-bruised heart…

"She needs the elixir! She'll catch her death."

Since he didn't want to tell Mama why he didn't want to see Lucy—because he had fully expected to be indifferent and had been anything but—now might be a good time to explain viruses. But his explanation, he knew, would fall on deaf ears.

"She's a doctor's daughter. I'm sure she knows what she needs."

Mama looked stubborn.

"Mama, it's probably illegal to make this stuff, let alone dispense it."

She regarded him, her eyes narrow, and then without warning, "Are you speaking to your mother yet, *schatz?*"

He glared at her stonily.

"Nearly Mother's Day. Just two weeks away. She must be lonely for you."

The only thing his mother had ever been lonely for was her bank account. But he wasn't being drawn into this argument. And he could clearly see Mama had grabbed on to it now, like a dog worrying meat off a bone.

"How many years?" she asked softly, stubbornly.

He refused to answer out loud, but inside, he did the math.

"It's time," she said.

On this, and only this, he had refused her from

the first day he had come here. There would be no reconciliation with his mother.

"Just a card, to start," she said, as if they had not played out this scene a hundred times before. "I think I have the perfect one right here."

It was one of Mama's things. She always had a cupboard devoted to greeting cards. She had one suitable for every occasion.

Except son and mother estranged for fourteen years.

Without a word he picked up the bottle of home-made schnapps and went out the squeaking door. When he glanced back over his shoulder, Mama had her back to him, rummaging through the card cupboard, singing with soft satisfaction.

He noticed how hunched she was.

Frail, somehow, despite her bulk.

He noticed how badly the house needed repair, and felt guilty, again, that he had somehow let it get this bad.

Mac was not unaware that he had been back in Lindstrom Beach all of half an hour and all these uncomfortable feelings were rising to the surface. He didn't like feelings.

Lucy had been here when he had not. Well, he'd take over from her now.

It occurred to him that this trip was probably not going to be the quick turnaround he had hoped for. Still, a few days of intense work, and he'd be out of here, leaving all these uneasy feelings behind him.

"Make sure she drinks some," Mama shouted as the screen creaked behind him. "Make sure. Don't come back here unless she does."

And much as he didn't want Lucy to be right about anything, and much as he didn't like the unexpected feelings, he realized, reluctantly, she had been right to insist he come back here.

Mama needed him.

And yes, the time to honor his foster mother was definitely now. But he would leave the gala to Lucy, and honor his foster mother by making sure her house was livable before he left again.

CHAPTER FOUR

MAC CROSSED THE familiar ground between the two houses. He noted, again, that Lucy's property was everything Mama's was not. Even with the lawns melting together, the properties were very different: Mama's ringed in huge trees—that were probably hard to mow around—the Lindstrom place well-maintained, oozing the perfect taste of old money.

From the tidbits of information dropped by Mama, Mac knew Lucy had taken over the house from her mother a year or so ago. Hadn't there been something about a broken engagement?

How did she find time to do the work that it used to take an entire team of gardeners to do?

Unless she doesn't have a life.

Which, also from tidbits dropped by Mama,

Lucy didn't. She ran some kind of online book business. A life, yes, but not the life he had expected the most popular girl in high school would have ended up with.

I don't care, Mac told himself, but if he really didn't, would he even have to say that to himself?

He debated going to the front of the house, keeping everything nice and formal, but in the end, he stayed in the back and went across the deck. He stopped and surveyed the house. The stately white paint was faded and peeling; a large patch of a sample paint color had been put up.

It was a pale shade of lavender. Several boards underneath it had samples of what he assumed would be trim color, ranging from light lilac to deep purple.

The paint color made him think he didn't know Lucy at all.

Which, of course, he didn't. She was no more the same girl she had been when he'd left than he was the same man. He became aware of the sound of water running inside the house, assumed Lucy was showering and was grateful for the reprieve from another encounter with her.

He wasn't a little kid anymore. And neither was Lucy. He respected Mama, but he couldn't take her every wish as a command. *Make sure she drinks it.* Lucy could find the bottle and make up her own mind whether to drink it.

He would take his chances. If he didn't return for a while, Mama might not question how he had completed his assignment. And, hopefully, she would be off the topic of his mother by then, as well.

Mac set Mama's offering at Lucy's back door, and then strolled down to her dock to look over the canoes. They weren't particularly good quality—different ages and makes and colors. Then he saw a sign, fairly new, nailed to a wharf post like the one that had broken at Mama's.

Lucy's Lakeside Rentals. It outlined the rates and rules for renting canoes.

Lucy was renting canoes? He *really* didn't know her anymore. In fact, it almost seemed as if their roles were reversed. He had arrived, he knew every success he had ever hoped for, and she was mowing lawns and scraping together pennies by renting canoes.

He thought he should feel at least a moment's satisfaction over that. A little gloating from the kind of guy Lucy could never fall for might be in order. But instead, Mac felt oddly troubled. And hated it that he felt that way.

He looked at the house. He could still hear water running. He eased a canoe up with his toe. The paddles were stored underneath it.

Then Mac maneuvered the canoe off the dock and into the water, got into it and began to paddle toward the other side of the lake.

Even more than Mama's embrace, the silent canoe skimming across the water filled him with what he dreaded most of all—a sense of having missed this place, a sense that even as he had tried to leave it all behind him, this was home.

An hour later, eyeing Lucy's house for signs of life and relieved to find none, Mac put the canoe back on the dock. He felt like a thief as he crept up to her back door. The elixir was gone. He could report to Mama with a clear conscience. Still, the feeling of being a thief was not relieved by sticking twenty bucks under a rock to cover the rental of the canoe.

"Hey," Lucy cried, "Wait!"

He turned and looked at her, put his hands into his pockets. He looked annoyed and impatient.

"What are you doing?" Lucy called.

"I took one of your canoes out. There's rental money under the rock." This was said sharply, as if it was obvious, and she was keeping him from something important.

"I never said you could rent my canoe."

"I have to pass a character test?"

Below the sarcasm, incredibly, Lucy thought she detected the faintest thread of hurt. After all these years, could it still be between them?

I could never fall for a boy like you.

No, he was successful and worldly, and it was

written in every line of his stance that he didn't give a hoot what she thought of him.

"I didn't say that. You can't just take a canoe."

"I didn't just take it. I paid you for it."

"You need to tell me where you're going. What if you didn't come back?"

"I've been paddling these waters since I was fourteen. I've kayaked some of the most dangerous waters in the world. I think I can be trusted with your canoe."

Trust. There it was again. The missing ingredient between them.

"It's not the canoe I'm worried about. I need to give you a life jacket."

"You're worried about me, Lucy Lin?" Now, aggravatingly, he was pulling out the charm to try to disarm her.

"No!"

"So what's the problem?"

"You should have asked."

"Maybe I should have. But we both know I'm not the kind of guy who does things by the book."

Again she thought she heard faint challenge, a hurt behind the mocking tone.

She sighed. "I don't want your money, Mac. If you want to take a canoe, take one. But let someone know where you're going. At least Mama, if you don't want to talk to me."

She was unsettled to realize now she was the one who felt hurt. Not that she had a right to be. Of course he wouldn't want to talk to her. She'd pushed him into the lake. Though she had a feeling his aversion to her went deeper than that recent incident.

"I don't need your charity," he said, "I'd rather pay you."

"Well, I don't need your charity, either."

"You know what? I'll just have my own equipment sent up."

"You do that."

She watched him walk away, his head high, and felt regret. They needed to talk about Mama, if nothing else. But he hadn't returned her calls, and he didn't want to talk to her now, either.

Lucy picked up his twenty-dollar bill, stuck it in an envelope, scrawled his name across it. Not bothering to dress, she crossed the lawns between the two houses in her housecoat, but didn't knock on the door.

She followed his lead. She put the envelope under a rock and walked away. When she got home, she inspected the canoes, saw which one he had been using, and shoved a life jacket underneath it.

"What's this?" Mama said, handing him the envelope.

Mac looked in it and sighed with irritation. Trust Lucy. She was always going to have the last word.

Except this time she wasn't, damn her. He folded the envelope, tucked it in his pocket and went out the back door. The last person he would ever accept charity from was Lucy. He owed her for the canoe, fair and square, and the days of her—or anyone in this town—feeling superior to him were over.

He lifted his hand to knock on her back door to return the money to her. Raised voices drifted out the open French doors and he moved away from the paint and peered into Lucy's house.

"You're wrecking the neighborhood!" someone said shrilly.

"It's just a sample." That voice was Lucy's, low and conciliatory.

"Purple? You're going to paint your house purple? Are you kidding me? It's an absolute monstrosity. When Billy and I saw it from the boat the other day, I nearly fell overboard."

Lucy had a perfect opportunity to say, *too bad you didn't,* but instead she defended her choice.

"I thought it was funky."

"Funky? On Lakeshore Drive?"

No answer to that.

Mac tried the door, and it was unlocked. He pulled it open and slid in. After a moment, his eyes adjusted to being inside and he saw Lucy at her front door, still wrapped in a housecoat, her hands folded defensively over her chest, looking up at a taller woman, the other woman's slenderness of the painful variety.

Now, there was a face from the past. Claudia Mitchell-Franks. Dressed in a trouser suit he was going to guess was linen, her makeup and hair done as if she was going to a party. Her thin face was pinched with rage.

Lucy was everything Claudia was not. Freshscrubbed from the shower, her short hair was towel-ruffled and did not look any more sophisticated than it had fresh out of the drink. She was nearly lost inside a white housecoat, the kind that hung on the back of the bathroom door in really good hotels.

Her feet were bare, and absurdly that struck him as far sexier than her visitor's stiletto sandals.

"And don't even think you're renting canoes this year! Last summer it increased traffic in this area to an unreasonable level, and you don't have any parking. The street above your place was clogged. And I had riffraff paddling by my beach."

"There's no law against renting canoes," Lucy said, but without much force.

This was the same Lucy who had just pushed him into the water? Why wasn't she telling old Claudia to take a hike?

"I had one couple stop and set up a picnic on my front lawn!" Claudia snapped.

"Horrors," Lucy said dryly. He found himself rooting for her. *Come on, Lucy, you can do better than that.*

"I am not spending another summer explaining to people it's a private beach," Claudia said.

Shrilly, too, he was willing to bet.

"It isn't," Lucy said calmly. "You only own to the high-water mark, which in your case is about three feet from your gazebo. Those people have a perfect right to picnic there if they want to."

Mac felt a little unwilling pride in her. That was information he'd given her all those years ago when he'd thumbed his nose at all those people trying to claim they owned the beaches.

"I hope you don't tell *them* that," Claudia said.

"I have it printed on the brochure I give out at rental time," she said, but then backtracked. "Of course I don't. But can't we share the lake with others?"

The perfectly coiffed Claudia looked as if she was going to have apoplexy at the idea of sharing the lake. Mac was pretty sure Claudia was one of the girls who used to sit on that deck painting her toenails while the "riffraff" slaved in the yard.

"Well, you won't be giving out any brochures this year, no, you won't! You'll need a permit to run your little business. And you're not getting one. And you know what else? You can forget the yacht club for your fund-raiser."

"I've already paid my deposit," Lucy said, clearly rattled.

"I'll see that it's returned to you."

"But I have a hundred confirmed guests coming. The gala is only two weeks away!" There was a pleading note in her voice.

"This is what you'll be up against if you even try rezoning. This is a residential neighborhood. It always has been and it always will be."

"That's what this is really about, isn't it?"

"We finally no longer have to put up with the endless parade of young thugs next door to this house, and you do this?"

He'd heard enough. He stepped across the floor.

"Lucy, everything okay here?"

Lucy turned and looked at him. He could see her eyes were shiny, and he hoped he was the only person in the room who knew that meant she was close to tears.

He thought she might be angry that he had barged into her house, but instead he saw relief on her delicate features as he approached her. Despite the brave front, he could tell that for some reason she felt as if she was in over her head. Maybe because this attack was coming from someone who used to be her friend?

"You remember Claudia," she said.

He would have much rather Lucy told Claudia to get the hell out of her house instead of politely making introductions.

Claudia was staring at him meanly. Oh, boy, did he ever remember that look! The first time he'd taken Lucy out publicly, for an ice cream cone on Main Street, they had run into her, and she'd had that same look on her skinny, malicious face.

"I know you," she said tapping a hard, bloodred-lacquered fingernail against a lip that matched.

He waited for her to recognize him, for the mean look to deepen.

Instead, when recognition dawned in her eyes, her whole countenance changed. She smiled and rushed at him, blinked and put her claw on his arm, dug her talon in, just a little bit.

"Why, Macintyre Hudson." She beamed up at him. "Aren't you the small-town boy who has done well for himself?"

He told himself he should find this moment

exceedingly satisfactory, especially since it had happened in front of Lucy. Instead, he felt a sensation of discomfort—which Lucy quickly dispelled.

Because behind Claudia, Lucy crossed her arms over her chest and frowned. Then she caught his eye and pantomimed gagging.

He didn't want to be charmed by Lucy, but he couldn't help but smile. Claudia actually thought it was for her. He didn't let the impression last. He slid out from under her fingertips.

"I seem to remember being one of the young thugs from next door. *And* the riffraff who had the nerve to paddle by your dock. I might even have had the audacity to eat my lunch on your beach now and again."

She hee-hawed with enthusiasm. "Oh, Mac, such a sense of humor! I've always *adored* you. My kids—I have two boys now—won't wear anything but Wild Side. If it doesn't have that little orangey kayak symbol on it, they won't put it on."

He tried not to show how appalled he was that his brand was the choice of the elite little monkeys who lived around the lake.

"What brings you home?" Claudia purred.

Over Claudia's bony shoulder, he saw Lucy now had her hands around her own neck, the internationally recognized symbol for choking. He tried to control the twitching of his lips.

"Lucy's having a party to honor my mother. I wouldn't have missed it for the world."

Considering that it had given him grave satisfaction to snub Lucy by giving the event a miss, this news came as a shock to him.

"Oh. That. I wasn't expecting *you* would come for *that*. There's been a teensy problem with location. Anyway, it's not as if she's your *real* mother."

Unaware how insensitive that remark was, Claudia forged ahead, her red lips stretched over teeth he found very large.

"I'm afraid the committee has voted to revoke our rental to Lucy. And we don't meet again until next month, and that's too late. But you know, the elementary-school gym is probably available. I'd be happy to check for you."

"No thanks."

"Don't be mad at *me*. It's really Lucy's fault. Norman Avalon is president of the yacht club this year. Do you remember him?"

An unpleasant memory of a boy throwing a partially filled Slurpee cup on him while he was shoveling three tons of mud out of a ditch came to mind.

"They live right over there. If Lucy paints the place purple, his wife, Ellen—you remember Ellen, she used to be a Polson—will have to look at it all day. She's ticked. Royally. And that was before the rezoning application. Macintyre, it is just sooo nice seeing you."

He didn't respond, tried not to look at Lucy, who had her eyes crossed and her tongue hanging out, her hands still around her own throat.

"Congrats on your company's success. I know Billy would love to see you if you have time. We generally have pre-dinner cocktails at the club on Friday."

Behind Claudia, Lucy dropped silently to her knees, and was swaying back and forth, holding her throat.

"The club?" As if there was only one in town, which there was.

"You know, the yacht club."

"Oh, the one Lucy isn't renting anymore. To honor *my* mother."

"Oh." With effort, since her expression lines had been removed with Botox, Claudia formed her face into contrite lines and lowered her voice sympathetically. "If you wanted to drop by on Friday and talk to Billy about it, he might be able to use his influence for *you.*"

Lucy keeled over behind her, her mouth moving in soundless gasping, like a beached fish.

"Billy who?"

"Billy. Billy Johnson. Do you remember him?"

"Uh-huh," he said, noncommittal. He seemed to remember smashing his fist into the face of the lovely Billy after he had made a guess about his heritage.

Claudia held up a hand with an enormous set of rings on it. "That's me now, Mrs. Johnson. Don't forget—cocktails. We dress, by the way."

"As opposed to what?"

"Oh, Mac, you card, you. Toodle-loo, folks."

She turned and saw Lucy lying on the ground, feigning death.

She stepped delicately over her inert body, and hissed, "Oh, for God's sake, Lucy, grow up. This man's the head of a multimillion-dollar company."

And she was gone, leaving a cloying cloud of perfume in her wake.

For a moment Lucy actually looked as if she'd allowed Claudia's closing barb to land. Her eyes looked shiny again. But then, to his great relief, she giggled.

"Oh, for God's sake, Lucy," he said sternly, "grow up."

She giggled more loudly. He felt his defenses

falling like a fortress made out of children's building blocks. He gave in to the temptation to play a little.

"Hey, I'm the head of a multimillion-dollar company. A little respect."

And then she started to laugh, and he gave in to the temptation a little more, and he did, too. It felt amazingly good to laugh with Lucy.

"You are good," he sputtered at her. "I got it loud and clear. Charades. Three words. *She's killing me.*"

He went over, took her hand and pulled her to her feet. She collapsed against him, laughing, and for the second time that day he felt the sweetness of her curves in his arms.

"Mac," she cooed, between gasps of laughter. "I've always *adored* you."

"The last time you looked at me like that, I got pushed in the lake."

She howled.

"What was that whole horrid episode with

Claudia about?" he finally said, putting her away from him, wiping his eyes.

The humor died in her eyes. "Apparently if you even think of painting your house purple, you're off the approved list for renting the yacht club."

He had a sense that wasn't the whole story between the two women, but he played along.

"Boo-hoo," he said, and they were both laughing again.

"I haven't laughed like that for a long time."

She hadn't? Why? Suddenly, protecting himself did not seem quite as important as it had twenty minutes ago when he had come across her lawn to give her her money back.

"It's really no laughing matter," Lucy said, sobering abruptly. "Now I've gone and ticked her off—"

"Royally," he inserted, but she didn't laugh again.

"And I've got a caterer coming from Glen Oak, but they have to have a kitchen that's been food-safe certified. The school won't do."

"Don't worry. We'll fix it."

"We?" she said, raising an eyebrow at him, but if he wasn't mistaken she was trying valiantly not to look relieved.

"I told Claudia I came back for the party."

"But you didn't."

"When I saw Mama's place falling down, I realized I might be here a little longer than I first anticipated."

"Her place *is* in pretty bad repair," Lucy said. "I was shocked by it when I first came home. I've done my best."

"Thanks for that. I appreciate it. But don't quit your day job."

"She would love it if you were here for a while. Being at the gala would be a bonus. For her, I mean."

Mama *would* love it. But staying longer than he'd anticipated was suddenly for something more than getting Mama's house back in order. When he'd seen that barracuda taking a run at Lucy, he'd felt protective.

He didn't want to feel protective of Lucy. He wanted to hand her her money and go. He wanted to savor the fact she was on the outs with her snobbish friends.

But he was astonished to find that not only was he not gloating over Lucy's fall from grace, he felt as if he couldn't be one more bad thing in her day. Mama Freda would be proud: despite his natural inclination to be a cad, he seemed to be leaning toward being a better man.

Lucy seemed to realize she was in her house-coat and inappropriately close to him. She backed off, and looked suddenly uncomfortable.

"Claudia is right. I'm embarrassed. What made me behave like that? You, I suppose. You've always brought out the worst in me."

"Look, let's get some things straight. Claudia is *never* right, and I *never* brought out the worst in you."

"You didn't? Lying to my parents? Sneaking out? You talked me into smoking a cigar once. I drank my first beer with you. I—" Her face clouded, and for a moment he thought she was going to mention the most forbidden thing of all, but she said, "I became the kind of girl no one wanted sitting in the front pew of the church."

"That would say a whole lot more about the church than the kind of girl you were. I remember you laughing. Coming alive like Sleeping Beauty kissed by a prince. Not that I'm claiming to be any kind of prince—"

"That's good."

"I remember you being like a prisoner who had been set free, like someone who had been bound up by all these rules and regulations learning to live by your own guidelines. And learning to be spontaneous. I think it was the very best of you."

"There's a scary thought," she said, running a hand through her short, rumpled hair, not looking at him.

"I think the seeds of the woman who would paint her house purple were planted right then."

"You like the color?" she asked hopefully. "You saw my sample when you came in, didn't you?"

He hated it that she asked, as if she needed someone's approval to do what she wanted. "It only matters if you like the color."

"I wish that were true," she said ruefully.

"I remember when you used to be friends with Mrs. Billy-Goat Johnson," he said.

"I know. But I think the statute of limitations has run out on that one, so I won't accept responsibility for it anymore." She tried to sound careless, but didn't quite pull it off.

Suddenly it didn't seem funny. Lucy had changed. Deeply. And that change had not been accepted by the people around her. He suspected it went a whole lot deeper than her painting her house purple.

Well, so what? People did change. He had changed, too. Though probably not as deeply. He tended to think he was much the same as he had always been, a self-centered adrenaline junkie, driven by some deep need to prove himself that no amount of success ever quite took away. In other words, when Lucy had called him a jerk she hadn't been too far off the mark.

The only difference was that now he was a jerk with money.

She had helped Mama when he had not, and for that, if nothing else, he was indebted to her.

But now Lucy seemed somehow embattled, as if she desperately needed someone on her side.

Not me, he told himself sternly. He wasn't staying here. He owed Lucy nothing. He was getting a few of the more urgent things Mama needed done cleared up. Okay, it wouldn't hurt to stay a few more days for Lucy's party. That would make Mama happy. It wasn't about protecting Lucy from that barracuda. Or maybe it was. A little bit. But tangling his life with hers?

It occurred to him that he may have lied to himself about his reasons for never coming back to Lindstrom Beach. He had told himself it was because it was the town that had scorned him. The traditional place full of Brady Bunch families, where he'd been the kid with no real family and a dark, secret history.

He'd played on that and developed a protective persona: adrenaline junkie, renegade, James Dean of the high-school set. It had brought a surprising fan base from some of the kids, though not their parents.

Not the snooty doctor's daughter, either. Not at first.

But now, standing here looking at Lucy, it occurred to him none of that was the reason he had avoided returning to this place.

Had he always known, at some level, that coming home again would require him to be a better man?

But would that mean looking out for the girl who had rejected him?

"May I use your phone?" he asked. "My cell got wrecked in the lake."

Her expression asked if he had to, she suddenly seemed eager to divest herself of him. But she looked around and handed him a cordless. Now that he had decided to be a better man, he was going to follow through before he changed his mind.

He could look at it as putting Claudia in her place as much as helping Lucy.

"Casey?" he said to his assistant. "Yeah, away for a few days... My hometown... You didn't know I had a hometown?... Hatched under a rock? Thanks, buddy." He waggled his eyebrows at Lucy, but she was pretending not to listen.

"Look, I need twenty thousand dollars of clothing products, sizes kid to teen, delivered to the food bank, boy's and girl's club and social services office of Lindstrom Beach, British Columbia. Make sure some of it gets to every agency that helps kids within a fifty-mile radius of that town...Yeah, giveaways.

"Of course you've never heard of Lindstrom Beach. When that's done—if you can have the whole area blanketed by tomorrow—take out a couple of ads on the local TV and radio stations thanking the Lindstrom Beach Yacht Club for donating their facilities for the Mother's Day Gala.

"Thanks, buddy. Don't know when I'll be back and don't bother with the cell. I made the mistake of not bringing the Wild Side waterproof case. Oh, throw some of those in with the other donations. I'll pick up another cell phone in the next few days."

Lucy was no longer pretending not to listen. She was staring at him as he found the button and turned off her phone. He handed it back to her. If he was not mistaken, she was struggling not to look impressed.

"Just admit it," he said. "That was great. Two birds with one stone."

"Everybody does not call you Mr. Hudson," she said, pleased. "Two birds?"

"Yeah. Claudia's stuck-up kids just became a whole lot less exclusive, and unless I miss my guess, you are *in* at the yacht club."

"You hate the yacht club," she reminded him.

"I've always had a strange hankering for anything anybody tells me I can't have."

Her arms folded more tightly over her chest and her eyes looked shiny again.

"I didn't mean you," he said softly.

"Let's not kid ourselves. That was part of the attraction. Romeo and Juliet. Bad boy and good girl."

"I don't think that was part of the attraction for me," he said, slowly. "It was more what I said before. It was watching you come into yourself, caterpillar to butterfly."

"Actually," she said, and she shoved her little nose in the air, reminding him of who she had been before he'd taught her you didn't go to hell for saying *damn*, "I don't want to have this discussion. In fact, if you don't mind, I need to get dressed."

"I have to give this to you first. Special delivery," he said, holding out the money to her. "What was that about rezoning?"

She ignored the envelope. "I think it had to do

with the canoes. I think you're supposed to re-zone to run a business."

But she suddenly wasn't looking at him. He was startled. Because, scanning her face, he was sure she was being deliberately evasive. What did renting canoes have to do with finally getting rid of the young thugs next door? Though it was Claudia they were dealing with. That was a leap in logic she could probably be trusted to make.

"I can put a lawyer on it if you want."

"I don't need you to fix things. I already told you I'm not in the market for a hero."

"Take your money."

"No. Are you in my house without an invitation?" she asked, annoyed.

"Boy, I saved you from drowning *and* from Claudia, and your gratitude, in both instances, seems to be almost criminally short-lived."

"Oh, well," she said.

"Anyone could come in your house without an invitation. You should consider locking the back door at least."

"Don't you dare tell me what to do! This is not the big city. And don't show up here after all these years and think you are going to play big brother. I don't need one."

But it was evident from what he had just seen that she needed something, someone in her court. Still, he was no more eager to play big brother to her than she was to cast him in that role.

But again, if that was what being a better man required of him, he'd suck it up. No looking at her lips, though. Or at the place her housecoat was gapping open slightly, revealing the swell of a deliciously naked breast.

"Lindstrom Beach may not be the big city," he said, reaching out and gently pulling her housecoat closed. "But it's not the fairy tale you want to believe in, either."

She glanced down, slapped his hand away, and held her housecoat together tightly with her fist. "As a matter of fact, I gave up on fairy tales a long time ago."

"You did?" he said skeptically.

"I did," she said firmly.

He looked at her more closely, and there was that subtle anger in her again suddenly. He missed the girl who had lain on the floor, clutching her throat. He also felt the little ripple of unease intensify—the one that had started when he saw her clumsy repair job in Mama's porch. It was true. There was something very, very different about her.

In high school she had been confident, popular, perky, smart, pretty. She'd been born with a silver spoon in her mouth and had the whole world at her feet. Her crowd, including Claudia, expected it that way.

But Claudia had always had a certain hard smoothness to her, like a rock too polished. In Lucy, he remembered a certain dewy-eyed innocence, a girl who really did believe in Prince Charming, and for some of the happiest moments of his life, had mistakenly believed it was him.

But Lucy Lindstrom no longer had the look of a woman waiting for her prince.

In fact, from behind the barrier of her newly closed housecoat, she looked stubborn and offended. So, she did not want a hero. Or a prince. Good for her. And he was not looking for a damsel in distress. Or a princess.

So they were safe.

Except, he didn't really feel safe. He felt some danger he couldn't identify, so heavy in the air he might be able to taste it, the same way a deer could taste a threat on the wind.

"What happened to your fiancé?" he asked.

"What fiancé?"

"Mama told me you were going to get married."

"I changed my mind."

"She told me that, too."

"But she didn't give you the details?"

"No. Why would she know the details?"

"You're not from around these parts, are you, son?" She did a fairly good impression of a well-known TV doctor.

"I don't know what you mean."

"My engagement breakup was front-page news

after my fiancé was chased naked down a quiet residential street in Glen Oak by a gun-wielding man who just happened to be the cuckolded husband of a woman who was my friend and the barista in our bookstore coffee shop."

It seemed Lucy Lindstrom's fall from grace had been complete. Mac ordered himself to feel satisfied. But that wasn't what he felt at all. He couldn't even pretend.

"Aw, Lucy." Her eyes had that shiny look again. He wanted to reach for her and hold her, but he knew if he did she would never forgive him.

"Don't feel sorry for me, please." She held up her hand. "Everything is on film these days. Someone caught the whole thing on their phone camera. It was a local sensation for a few days."

"Aw, Lucy," he said again, his distress for her genuine.

"Aren't you going to ask me if I never guessed something was going on? Everyone else asks that."

"No, I'm going to ask you if you want me to track him down and kill him."

"With your bare hands?" she asked, and though her voice was silky her eyes were shining again.

"Is he the one who made you quit believing in fairy tales?"

"No, Mac," she said quietly. "That happened way before him."

Her eyes lingered for just a moment on his lips, and then she licked hers, and looked away.

Mac turned from the sudden intensity, and made himself focus on the house—anything but her lips and the terrible possibility it was him who had made her stop believing in fairy tales.

"This isn't how I remember it."

Once, he had made the mistake of going to the front door when she was late meeting him at the dock for a canoe trip.

He'd stepped inside and it had reminded him of an old castle: dim and grim, the front room so crowded with priceless antiques that it felt hard to breathe. He found out he'd been invited inside to get a piece of her father's mind, and that's when he'd discovered that Lucy had been seeing him on the sly.

I forbid you to see my daughter.

After all these years Mac wasn't sure, but the word *riffraff* might have come into play. Of course, being *forbidden* to see Lucy had only made him come up with increasingly creative ways to spend time with her.

And it had intensified the pleasure of sneaking into this very room, when her parents were asleep upstairs, and kissing her until they had both been breathless with longing.

That first meeting with her father had been nothing in comparison to the last one.

There's been a rash of break-ins around the lake. My house is about to be broken into. The police are going to find the stolen goods next door, in your bedroom. You'll be arrested and it will be the final straw for that rotten place. I've always wanted to buy it. Someday, Lucy and the man she marries will live there.

Mac had known for a long time that he had to go. That there was no future for him in Lindstrom Beach and never would be.

He'd told her about her father's threat and said he couldn't stand it in this town for one more second. And that's when she had said it.

I could never fall for a boy like you.

Had her father convinced her he was a thief? That he was behind the break-ins that had happened that summer?

Or had she just come to her senses and realized it wasn't going to work? That a guy like him was never going to be able to give a girl like her the things she had become accustomed to?

It seemed to him that there was a lot of space between them that was too treacherous to cross. They'd caused each other pain, he was sure, but he was sure he had caused her more than she had caused him.

Maybe he had been the one who wrecked fairy tales for her.

But he'd already been a world away from fairy tales by the time he met her.

Safer to focus on the here and the now.

"There used to be a wall here," he said. *And a couch here*. He decided that focusing on the here and now meant not mentioning the couch. Not even thinking about it would have been good, too, but it was too late for that.

"My mom actually opened the walls ups after my dad died."

Which meant they were not, technically, even in the same room they had once made out in. The ghosts of their younger selves, breathless with need, were not here.

Mac somehow doubted her mother had achieved the almost tangible quality of sanctuary that the room had. Her mother, as he recalled her, had been much like Claudia. This room would have had the benefit of an interior designer, the magazine-shoot-perfect layout. It would have been designed with an eye for entertaining. And impressing.

But Lucy had created a space that was casual

and inviting. It was a place where a person could read a book or stay in their housecoat all day. But there was something about it that he couldn't quite put his finger on.

Mac went through to the dining-room table to set down the envelope of money. There were papers stacked neatly on it. It was not the space of someone who entertained or had large dinner parties. He put his finger on it: her space had a feeling of surprising solitude clinging to it.

Lucy? Who had been at the heart of a crowd, directing all the action, without even knowing she was? Imposing her standards on others as unconsciously as breathing?

Lucy? Who had been the most popular girl in her graduating class, not standing up for herself with the likes of Claudia Mitchell-Franks?

Lucy? Who had always been "in," now suddenly having to beg for use of the yacht club in the town named for her grandfather?

Lucy? Who had been as conservative as her parents before her, now tentatively painting her house purple and enraging the community by running a commercial venture from her dock?

"What happened to you?" he asked softly.

And he saw more than secrets in her eyes— enormous, green, dazzling. But if he didn't allow himself to be dazzled, he was sure he saw something he really didn't want to see. He saw fear.

CHAPTER FIVE

FOR ONE MOMENT Lucy was almost overcome by a desire to tell him. Everything. That after he had left that summer, her whole world as she had known it had changed irrevocably and forever.

But she was not giving in to impulses—she already regretted the charade behind Claudia's back—and especially not where Mac was concerned.

"Nothing happened to me. I grew up. That's all."

She didn't want him to look too closely at the table. The charitable foundation registration was sitting there. So was the rezoning application that would allow her to turn this house into a group home for unwed mothers.

She was not getting into that. Not with him. Not now and not ever.

Still clutching her housecoat closed, she went over and inserted herself between him and her secrets.

"Is there something on that table you don't want me to see?"

She was close enough that she could smell him, the scent of the pure lake water not quite eradicated by a faint soapy scent.

"No."

"Unlike Claudia," he said, "you are developing a little worry furrow right here."

He touched between her brows.

And she wanted, weakly, to lean into his thumb and share her burdens. She had secrets. She was worrying. It was none of his business. He was a man she had known back when he was a boy. To think she knew anything about him now, on the basis of that, would be pure folly.

Unless she remembered she couldn't trust him.

"Seven years," he said, peering over her shoulder. "What could possibly be on your table after seven years that you wouldn't want me to see?"

He waggled his eyebrows at her in that fiendish way that he had. "The possibility of a lingerie catalog is making me look harder."

Enough. She snatched the money from where he had set it on the table, and looked at it with exaggerated interest. "I don't want this."

Mac shrugged. "Donate it to your favorite charity."

"All right," she said stiffly. There was an irony in that that he never had to know about. In fact, he did not need to know one more thing about her. She was all done laughing for the day. It felt like a total weakness that he coaxed that silly part from her. And the story of her broken engagement.

She didn't like how that had changed him, some wariness easing in him as he looked at her.

"Now, I have to go get dressed, so if you'll excuse me…"

"What *is* your favorite charity?"

She shook her head, felt put out that he was

trying to make conversation with her instead of obediently heading for the door.

"Why? Do you want the receipt?"

He turned, and relieved, Lucy thought that she had insulted him and he was going. Instead, he went into her living room and sat down in one of her overstuffed chairs. If she was not mistaken, the only reason he was still here was that he was devilishly enjoying her discomfort.

At least he'd moved away from the rezoning documents.

He appeared totally relaxed, deeply enjoying the view out her window.

She cocked her head at him, unforthcoming. Who could outwait whom?

He picked up the book that was open on the arm, but she raced over and snatched it away— not quickly enough.

"Interesting reading material for a girl who has given up on fairy tales. *To Dance with a Prince?*"

She bit back an urge to defend her choice of reading material, but he had already moved on.

"I like what you've done to the place," he said. "Kind of ski-lodge chic instead of Victorian manor house. I doubt that was your mom. I bet the exterior paint color wasn't her choice, either. It's surprisingly Bohemian for this neck of the woods."

"The paint is barely dry and the neighbors have lost no time in letting me know they don't appreciate me indulging my secret wild side."

And then it was there, the danger. It sizzled in the air between them. Her secret wild side was interwoven with their history. Those heated summer nights of discovery, bodies melting together. That hunger they'd had, an almost desperate sense of not being able to get enough of each other.

She found his eyes on her lips and the memory was scalding.

She was shocked by what she wanted. To be wild. To taste him just one more time. To throw caution to the wind.

"I would have pictured you in a very different life, Lucy."

"Really?"

"Traditional. A big house. A busy husband. A vanload of kids, girls who need to get to ballet lessons, boys who need to be persuaded not to keep their frogs in the kitchen sink."

She was silent.

"I thought you would be living a life very similar to that of your parents, that you'd be hanging with all those kids you grew up with. Friday drinks with friends at the yacht club, water-skiing on weekends in the summer, trips to the ski hill in the winter."

She arched an eyebrow at him. "I'm surprised you pictured me at all."

It was his turn to be silent. The view out the window seemed to hold his complete attention. And then he said, quietly, "A man never forgets his first love."

Something trembled inside her. "I didn't know I was your first love."

"How could you not know? Those crazy weeks, Lucy. I'd wake up thinking of you. I'd go to sleep thinking of you. We spent every moment we could together. It felt as if I couldn't breathe unless you were there to give me air."

How well she remembered the intensity of those few weeks.

"You never said you loved me," she whispered.

He looked at her and smiled. She distrusted that smile. It could still turn her insides to jelly. That devil-may-care smile made him the most handsome man alive, but it said that nothing mattered to him. It was the wall he put up.

"I never say I love anyone," he said. "Not even Mama."

"You've never told Mama you love her?"

"I don't think so."

"Well, that just stinks."

"Anyway, those days are a long way behind us, Lucy."

Yes, they were and it would do nothing but harm to dredge them up. Even now, she could feel her heart beating way too quickly at his admission that he had spent night and day doing nothing but thinking of her. At the time, he certainly hadn't let on that's what was going on for him!

"So, what does the grown-up Lucy do for fun?"

The question took her aback. "Fun?" she asked uncomfortably.

"You were the girl at the center of the fun, as hokey and wholesome as I found it at the time. The water fight on the front lawn of the high school. The fund-raising car wash where they shut down Main Street and brought out the fire truck. The three-day bike excursion to Bartlett. The canoe trip across the lake, camping on the Point.

"I remember standing over at Mama's one night when you had a group of kids here at your fire pit. You know what I couldn't believe? You had them all singing! All these kids who considered themselves cooler than cool, singing *Row Row Row Your Boat*."

"I thought those days were a long way behind

us," she muttered. "Besides, you never partici-
pated in any of those things!"

"No, I didn't."

"Why?"

"I felt I didn't fit in."

It was an admission of something real about
him, and for the second time Lucy was startled.
He had never once said anything like that when
they were together. He had revealed more about
himself in the last ten minutes than he had the
whole time they were together.

"That never showed," she said. "You always
seemed so supremely confident. Everybody
thought you were so cool. Unafraid, somehow.
Bold. If you wore a pair of jeans with a rip in the
knee, half the school had ripped their jeans by
the next week."

"It wasn't that I didn't have the right stuff—the
clothes, the great bike, though I didn't—it wasn't
that. It was that your crowd was all so damn *normal*. Two parents. Nice houses. A dog. Allow-
ances. Born into expectations of how they would

behave and what they would become. I felt excluded from that. Like I could never belong, only be a visitor."

"I hope I never made you feel like that."

"No, Lucy, you never did. In fact, for those few weeks—" He stopped.

"For those few weeks what?" she breathed.

But he rolled his shoulders, like a fighter shrugging off a blow. "Nothing."

And the veil was down over his eyes, and that was what she remembered most about him. Get close, but not too close.

"You kind of bucked all those expectations of you, didn't you, Lucy?"

Oh, yeah. Because she had had one life before Mac and a completely different one after.

"My life may not be what my father and mother expected, but I have a really good life. I love what I do."

"Mama keeps me posted."

She felt mortified, and he saw it and laughed.

"Don't worry, nothing juicy, just tidbits of

news. I heard about your online bookstore, and according to Mama, you do very well at it, too."

"Ah, well," Lucy said, wryly self-deprecating, "You know Mama. When she loves you, you can do no wrong."

"When did you two become so close? When I lived here there was always a kind of barrier, imposed by the doctor, between your family and her. You and Mama were polite to each other, and good neighbors, but you weren't mowing her lawn or repairing her house."

Again, Lucy had to fight with a voice inside her that said, *Wouldn't it be nice to tell him?*

But she reminded herself, firmly, that that summer when she had loved him, she had given and given and given until she had not a secret left. And he had not divulged anything about himself. Laughing at her efforts to find out.

I killed a man. With my bare hands.

"I don't remember the exact details," she lied. But oh, she remembered them so clearly. Flying across that lawn in the dark, the emotional pain in her so great, she was unaware she had stepped on a sharp rock and her foot was bleeding.

The door opening and Mama standing there.

Liebling! *What is it?*

"So, to get back to my original question, what do you do for fun?"

"My work's fun," she said firmly.

"I hope you're joking."

She felt mutinous. "What do you do for fun?"

"My work *is* fun. I developed a company that's all about fun. I think the roots of Wild Side started right here."

"So, your work is what you do for fun, too."

"Touché," he said. "But I do love the white-water kayaking. It is so physical and requires such intense concentration. It makes me feel more alive than just about anything I've ever done."

But a sudden memory flashed through his eyes and it was as if she could see it, too: lying in the sand beside him, the moonlight bathing them, never having ever felt quite so alive as that before.

Or since.

"I guess that's what I'm asking, Lucy. What makes you feel like that?"

"Like what?' she stammered.

"The way I feel when I am in a kayak. Alive. Totally engaged. Intensely in the moment. What makes you feel like that?"

If she said nothing, he would think she was a total loser. And in fact there was something that made her feel exactly like that.

"I have something," she said reluctantly. And she did. "It makes me feel alive, but I'm pretty sure you wouldn't call it fun."

"Try me."

"Not today." To tell him would just make her feel way too vulnerable.

"Drink the schnapps and I'll ask again."

She marched into her kitchen, got down a shot glass, filled it from Mama's bottle and went back out. She slammed the liquid back. She blinked hard.

"Okay," he said. "What do you do for fun, Lucy Lin?"

"You already figured it out," she said, "I work. Now, shoo. Because I have a lot of that to do today."

Shoo. She wished she had worded that differently. He looked way too closely at her. He was too close to striking a nerve.

He turned to go. "I'll be back."

"I was afraid you would say that," she muttered as she watched him go. Even though she ordered herself not to, even though she knew she shouldn't, Lucy went and watched him cross the yards back to Mama's house.

He was whistling and the melody drifted in her open door, mingled with the scent of the trees, and tingled along her spine.

Rebel. It was a warning if she had ever heard one, and yet Lucy was aware that she felt alive in ways she had not for a long, long time.

Mac went back across the lawns, pensive. Something was so different about Lucy. What had changed in her?

He got the sense that maybe she had become an outcast from the Lindstrom Beach crowd, which was the most surprising thing of all.

As surprising as her mowing lawns and trying to fix floorboards and renting canoes.

Her new aloneness in this community, was it her choice or theirs?

What mattered, really, was that Lucy was shouldering all that responsibility for Mama and he had let her. She seemed alone, and she seemed just a little too grim about life.

Somewhere in her was a woman who wanted to paint her house purple, and probably wasn't going to.

Without an intervention. He was going to be the man Mama expected him to be.

Before he left here, he was going to help Lucy have some fun.

Lucy actually felt light-headed.

It was the schnapps, she told herself, not Mac Hudson crash-landing in her world. She went back upstairs and looked at herself critically in her bedroom's full-length mirror. First soaking wet, now in her housecoat! These were not the impressions she had intended!

She had intended to look sophisticated and coolly professional. Even if she did have a job where she could work in her pajamas if she wanted to.

Lucy found herself dressing for the potential of another meeting with him, and then made herself get to work. First, she turned on her computer and reviewed orders that had come in overnight. There were also a dozen more RSVPs for the Mother's Day Gala, three of them from girls she had gone to high school with, saying "will NOT be able to attend."

She felt something sag within her, and told herself it was not disappointment. It was pragmatic: the people refusing to come were the ones who could make the best donations to her cause.

But, of course, her cause was at odds with their vision for life around the lake.

Lucy forced herself to think of something else. She went into a spare room that had become the book room, retrieved the book orders and began to package them.

Later, she would review her rezoning proposal for Caleb's House, the documents lying out on her dining room table where she hadn't wanted Mac to see them.

As the day warmed, Lucy moved out onto her deck to work, as she often did. She told herself it was a beautiful day, but was annoyed at herself for sneaking peeks at Mama's house.

She could hear enormous activity—saws and hammers—but she didn't see Mac.

She wanted to go see what he was doing over there, but pride made her stay at home.

When she had finally succeeded in putting him out of her mind, the radio was on and she heard the ad about the donation of the Wild Side clothing in thanks for the donation of the yacht club for the Mother's Day Gala.

Within an hour she had been phoned by several representatives of the yacht club—notably not Claudia—falling all over themselves to make sure she knew she was most welcome to the space for the Mother's Day Gala, and that the regular charge had been waived.

Now, as evening fell, Lucy was once again cozy in her pajamas, trying to concentrate on a movie. She found herself resentful that he was next door. She and Mama often watched a movie or a television show together in the evenings.

She hated it that she felt lonely. She hated it that she was suddenly looking at her life differently.

When had she allowed herself to become so boring? Her phone rang.

"Hello, Lucy."

"Mac," she said. "I've been meaning to call and thank you. The yacht club has confirmed."

He snickered. So did she.

"You didn't tell me Mama's car isn't even insured."

"Why would she insure a car she can't drive?"

"I took it to town three times for building materials before she remembered to tell me, ever so casually, that the insurance had lapsed. I could have been arrested!"

From loneliness to this: laughter bubbling up inside her.

"Anyway, Mama would like to see a movie tonight. Can you drive me to town so I can get one for her?"

"You're welcome to borrow my car anytime you need one."

"I'll keep that in mind, thanks, but Mama says I'm not allowed to pick a movie without you there. She says I'll bring home something awful. A man movie, she called it. You know. Lots of action. Blood. Swearing."

"Yuck."

"Just what Mama said. On the other hand, if we send you to get a movie without me, it'll probably be a two-hanky special, heavy on the violin music."

"Why don't you and Mama go get the movie?"

"She's making *apfelstrudel*." He sighed happily. "She says it's at the delicate stage. It'll be ready by the time we bring the movie back. She says you have to come have some."

It was one of Mama's orders. Unlike an invitation, you could not say no. As if anyone could say no to Mama's strudel, anyway. Still, it was not as if Lucy was agreeing to spend time with him. Or plotting to spend time with him. It was just happening.

"She hasn't stopped cooking since you got there, has she?"

"No, because I also made a grocery run before I found out I was driving illegally. She made schnitzel for supper," he said happily. "You know something? Mama's schnitzel would be worth risking arrest for. She's already started a new grocery list. Would you mind if we picked up a few things while we're in for the movie?"

Lucy did mind. She minded terribly that she had been feeling sorry for herself and lonely, and that now she wasn't. That life suddenly seemed to tingle with possibility.

From going for a movie and to the grocery store.

Her life *had* become too boring.

Of course, she wasn't kidding herself. The tingle of possibility had nothing to do with the movie or groceries.

Sternly, Lucy reminded herself she was not a teenager anymore. Back then, being around Mac had seemed like pure magic. But she'd been innocent. As he had pointed out earlier, she had believed in fairy tales. She'd been a hopeless romantic and a dreamer and an optimist.

It would be good to see how Mac fared with her adult self! It would be good to do a few ordinary things with him. Certainly that would knock him down off the pedestal she had put him on when she was nothing more than a kid. It would be good to see how her adult self fared around Mac.

It was like a test of all her new intentions, and Lucy planned on passing it!

"Meet me in the driveway," she said. "In ten minutes."

Did she take extra care in choosing what to wear? Of course she did. It was only human that while she wanted to break her fascination with Mac, it would be entirely satisfying to see his with her increase.

She wanted to be the one in the power position for a change.

If she looked at her life that was the whole problem. She had always given away too much power to others. Fallen all over herself trying to win approval.

If she had a fatal flaw, it was that she had mistaken approval for love.

"You know," Mac said, a few minutes later, "they say that people's choice of cars says a lot about them."

Lucy looked at her car, a six-year-old compact in an almost indistinguishable color of gray.

She frowned. The car was almost a perfect reflection of the life she seemed to be newly reassessing. "It's reliable," she said defensively.

"I can cross driving off the list of things you do for fun."

"What do you drive?"

"What do you think?" he said.

"I'm guessing something sporty that guzzles up more than your fair share of the world's resources!"

"You'd be guessing right, then. I have two vehicles. One a sports car and the other an SUV great for hauling equipment around."

"Both bright red?" she asked, not approvingly.

"Of course. One's a convertible. You'd like it."

"Flashy," she said.

"I don't enjoy being flashy," he said without an ounce of sincerity. "I just want to find my vehicle in the parking lot. It's crowded in the big city."

They got in the car. She did not offer to let him drive. It wasn't that her car would be a disappointment after what he was accustomed to. It was that she was not letting him take charge. It was a small thing, but she hoped that it said something about her, too.

"I'm glad you came with me," he said after her disapproving silence about his flashy car lengthened between them.

Something in her softened. What was the point of being annoyed at him? He wanted to be with her. She ordered her heart to stop. She glanced at him, and he was frowning at the list.

"I didn't want to have to ask a clerk where to find this." He held the list under her nose.

"Hey! I'm trying to drive."

It was a good reminder that the point of being annoyed with him was to protect herself.

"It's after seven. There's no traffic on this road." Still he withdrew the list. "C-u-m-i-n."

"Cumin?"

"I wouldn't have pronounced it like that. What is it, anyway?

"A spice."

He rapped himself on the forehead. "See? I thought it had something to do with feminine hygiene."

"Mac. You're incorrigible! What an awful thing to say!"

"Why are you smiling then?"

"My teeth are gritted. Do not mistake that for a smile! I do not find off-color remarks funny."

"Now you sound like you've been at finishing school with Miss Claudia. Don't take life so seriously, Lucy. It's over in a blink."

That was twice as annoying because she had said almost the very same thing to herself earlier. Lucy simmered in silence.

CHAPTER SIX

"SAME OLD PLACE," Mac said, as they entered the town on Lakeshore Drive, wound around the edge of the lake, through a fringe of stately Victorian houses, and then passed under the wooden arch that pronounced it Main Street.

Lucy's house was two miles—and a world— away from downtown Lindstrom Beach. Main Street had businesses on one side, quaint shops that sold antiques and ice cream and rented bicycles and mopeds. Bright planters, overflowing with petunias, hung from old-fashioned light standards.

On the other side of the street mature cottonwoods formed a boundary to the park. Picnic tables underneath them provided a shaded sitting area in the acres of white-sand beach that went to the water's edge.

"Charming," she insisted.

"Sleepy," he said. "No. Make that exhausted."

The shops would be open evenings in the peak of the summer season, but now they were closed, their bright awnings rolled up, outdoor tables and chairs put away against the buildings. There were two teenagers sitting at one of the picnic tables. She was pretty sure they were both wearing Wild Side shirts.

They left downtown and the main road bisected a residential area. Lucy Lindstrom loved her little town, founded by her grandfather. This part of it had wide tree-shaded boulevards, a mix of year-round houses and enchanting summer cottages.

Under the canopy of huge trees, in the dying light, kids had set up nets and were playing street hockey. They heard the cry of "car!" as the kids raced to get their nets out of the way.

"I bet you don't see that in the big city."

"See?" he said. "You still believe in the fairy tale."

"I don't really think it's so much a fairy tale," she said, a trifle defensively. "This town, my house, the lake, they give me a sense of sanctuary. Of safety. Of the things that don't change."

In a few weeks, as spring melted into summer, the lake would come alive. Main Street Beach, which Lucy could see from her dock, would be spotted with bright umbrellas, generations enjoying it together.

There would be plump babies in sun hats filling buckets with sand, mothers slathering sunscreen on their offspring and passing out sandy potato chips and drinks, grandmothers and grandfathers snoozing in the shade or lazily turning the pages of books.

Along Lakeshore Drive, boards would come off the windows of the summer houses. Power boats, canoes and the occasional plane would be tied up to the docks. The floats would be launched and quickly taken over by rowdy teenagers pushing and shoving and shouting. There would be the smell of barbecues and, later, sparks from bonfires would drift into a star-filled sky.

"I'm unchanging. As incorrigible as ever."

"Can you ever be serious?"

"I don't see the point."

"I love this town," she said, stubbornly staying on the topic of the town, instead of the topic of *him*. "How could anyone not love it?"

Now, added to that abundance of charm that was Lindstrom Beach, Lucy had her dream, and it was woven into the peace and beauty and values of her town. The dream belonged here, even if Claudia Johnson didn't think so!

And so did she. Even if Claudia Johnson disapproved of her.

"How could anyone not like it here?" She could have kicked herself as soon as it slipped out. It sounded suspiciously like she cared that he didn't like it here.

"How much you like Lindstrom Beach depends

on your pedigree." Suddenly he sounded very serious, indeed.

She glanced at him. His mouth had a firm line to it, and he took a pair of sunglasses out of his pocket and put them on. She was pretty sure those sunglasses had been in the lake yesterday.

"It does not."

"Spoken by the one with the pedigree. You have no idea what it was like to be a kid from the wrong side of the tracks in Lindstrom Beach."

This time the chill in the voice was hers. "That may be true, but it certainly wasn't for lack of trying."

Suddenly, the pain felt fresh between them, like fragile skin that had been burned only an hour or two before. He had been right. There was no point being so serious.

If she could, she would have left things as they were, lived contentedly in the lie that she was all over that, the summer she had spent loving Mac nothing more than the foolish crush of a woman barely more than a girl. She'd only been seventeen, after all.

He had teased her about it then. The perfect doctor's daughter having her walk on the wild side. When she had first heard the name of his company, she had wondered if he was taunting her for what she had missed. But he had never asked her to go on that journey with him. And besides, that brief walk on the wild side had been a mistake.

The repercussions had torn her oh-so-stable family apart. And then, there was the little place on a knoll behind the house, deeply shaded by hundred-year-old pines, that she went to, that reminded her what a mistake it had been.

Leave it, a voice inside her ordered. But she was not at all sure that she could.

"Macintyre Hudson," Lucy said, her voice deliberately reprimanding, "you lived next door to me, not on the wrong side of the tracks."

But underneath the reprimand, was she still hoping she could draw something out of him?

That she could do today what she had not been able to do all those years ago?

Find out who he really was, what was just beneath the surface of the incorrigible facade he put on for the world?

He snorted. "The wrong side of the tracks is not a physical division. Your father hated Mama's old cottage, hardly more than a fishing shack, being right next door to his mansion. He hated it more that she brought children of questionable background there. His failures in life: he failed to have Mama's place shut down, and he failed to bully her in to moving."

Mac didn't know that, in the end, her father had considered *her* one of his failures, too.

"But it looks like Claudia Johnson née Mitchell-Franks has taken over where he left off," he said drily. And then he grinned, as if he didn't care about any of it. "I think we should attend her little shindig on Friday night at the yacht club."

The grin back, she knew her efforts to get

below the surface had been thwarted. Again. She should have known better than to try.

"I wouldn't go there on Friday night if my life depended on it," she said.

"Really? Why?"

"First of all, I wasn't invited."

"You need an invitation?"

A little shock rippled through her. All those years ago, was it possible that he had never thought to invite her to go with him when he left Lindstrom Beach? That he had just thought if she wanted to go, she would have taken the initiative?

Lucy did not want to be thinking about ancient history. She was not allowing herself to dwell on what might have been.

But still, she said, "Yes, I need an invitation."

"Your grandfather built the damned place."

"I never renewed my membership when I came back."

"You're going to allow Claudia to snub you? I'd go just to tick her off. It could be fun."

But Lucy felt something dive in the bottom of her stomach at the thought of going somewhere where she wasn't wanted, all that old crowd looking at her as if she was the one who had most surprised them all, and not in a good way.

Fun. His diversionary tactic when anything got too serious, when anything threatened the fortress that was him.

"Well, showing up where I'm not wanted is not exactly my idea of a good time."

"I have a lot to teach you," he said, then, "And here we are at the grocery store. Which is open at—" he glanced at his watch "—half past seven. Good grief." He widened his eyes at her in pretended horror and whispered, "Lucy! Are they open Sunday?"

"Since I've moved back, yes."

"I'll bet there was a petition trying to make it close at five, claiming it would be a detriment to the town to have late-night and Sunday shopping. Ruin the other businesses, shut down the churches, corrupt the children."

She sighed. "Of course there was a petition."

The tense moment between them evaporated as he got out of the car and waited for her. "Come on, Lucy Lin, let's go find the cumin. And just for fun, we have to buy one thing that neither of us has ever heard of before."

"Would you quit saying the word *fun* over and over as if you don't think I know what it is? Besides, this is Lindstrom Beach, I don't think you'll find anything in this whole store that you've never heard of before."

"You're already wrong, because I'd never heard of cumin. Would you like to make a bet?"

Don't let him suck you into his world of irreverence, she ordered herself sternly.

"If I find something neither of us has ever heard of, you have to eat it, whatever it is," he challenged her.

"And if you don't?"

"You can pick something I have to eat."

It was utterly childish, of course. But, reluctantly she thought, it did seem like it might be fun. "Oh, goody. Pickled eggs for you."

"You remember that? That I hate those?"

Unfortunately, she remembered everything.

And suddenly it was there between them again, a history. An afternoon of canoeing, a picnic on an undeveloped beach on the far shore. Her laying out the picnic lunch she had packed with a kind of shy pride: basket, blanket, plates, cold chicken, drinks. And then the jar of eggs. Quail eggs, snitched from her mother's always well-stocked party pantry.

She had made him try one. He had made a big deal out of how awful it was. In fact, he had done a pantomime of gagging that surpassed the one she had done of Claudia yesterday. But, at that moment that he had started gagging on the egg, they had probably been going deeper, talking about something that mattered.

"I'm not worried about having to eat pickled eggs," he said. "I'm far too competitive to worry. I'll find something you've never heard of before.

Unlike you, who are somewhat vertically challenged, I am tall enough to see what they tuck away on the top shelves."

As he grabbed a grocery cart, Lucy desperately wanted to snatch the list from him and just do it the way she had always done it. Inserting playfulness into everyday chores seemed like the type of thing that could make one look at one's life afterwards and find it very mundane.

And with Mac? There was going to be an afterward, because he was restless and he would never be content in a place like this.

"Here's something now," he said, at the very first aisle. "Sasquatch Bread. I mean, really?"

"It's from a local bakery. It's Mama's favorite."

"We'll get some, then. How about this?" He picked up a container. *"Chapelure de blé?"*

"What?"

"I knew it. Here less than thirty seconds, and I've already won."

She looked at what he was holding. "You're reading the French side. It's bread crumbs."

"Trust the French to make bread crumbs sound romantic. We'll take some of these, too. You never know when you might need romantic bread crumbs."

She was not sure she wanted to be discussing romance with Mac, not even lightly, but the truth was he was hard to resist. Even complete strangers could see how irresistible he was. She did not miss the sidelong glance of a mother with a baby in her buggy or the cheeky smile of leggy woman in short shorts.

But it seemed as if his world was only about her. He didn't even seem to notice those other women, his focus so intent she could be giddy with it.

If she didn't know better than to steel herself.

But even with steeling herself against his considerable charm, just like that the most ordinary of things, shopping for groceries, was fun! He scoured the store for oddities, blowing dust from obscure items on the top shelves.

He thought he had her at quinoa, but when she

said she made a really good salad with it, that went in the cart, too.

The strangest thing was that she was in a grocery store that she had been in thousands of times. And it felt as if she was discovering a brand-new world.

"Got it," he finally said. He held out a large jar to her. "You have never heard of this!"

"Rolliepops," she read. "Pickled herring wrapped around a savory filling. Ugh!"

"Gotcha!"

He bought the largest size he could find, and they found the rest of the things on the list, plus items he deemed essential for movie night: popcorn, red licorice and chocolate-covered raisins.

"You are really going to enjoy snacking on your Rolliepops during the movie," he told her as they strolled out of the store with their laden cart.

"I'd rather eat the bread crumbs."

"Then you shouldn't have admitted you knew what they were. Retribution for the quail eggs all those years ago," he said happily as he stowed all the things he had bought—most of them not on the list and completely impractical—in the trunk of her car.

The video store was also fun as they wrangled over movies. This was the part of being with him that she had forgotten: it was easy.

It had always astonished both of them what good friends they became and how quickly. They had thought they would be opposites. Instead, they made each other laugh. They thought their worlds would be miles apart, instead they were comfortable in the new world they created.

And now it was as if seven years didn't separate them at all. She felt as if she had seen him just yesterday.

Finally, after much haggling, they settled on a romantic comedy.

By the time they got back, it never even occurred to Lucy not to join him at Mama's house for the movie and fresh strudel. They parked the car back in her driveway and walked over with the groceries.

The strudel was excellent, the movie abysmal, Mama got up halfway through it and went to bed.

Suddenly, they were alone. Too late, Lucy remembered what else had come so easily and naturally to them.

When they were alone, an awareness of each other tingled in the air between them.

Back then, they had explored it. She with guilt, he with hunger, both of them with a sense of incredible discovery. The memory of that made her ache with wanting.

He was so close. She could smell the familiar, intoxicating scent of him. If she reached out, she could touch his arm.

"I have to go," she said, jumping up abruptly.

"Something urgent to do? Feed your fish? Put up a new swatch of color?"

"Something like that," she said.

"Don't forget, you owe me. You still have to eat a Rolliepop."

She grimaced. "I think I'd have nightmares. Herring wrapped around something 'savory'?

Not my idea of a bedtime snack, but you know what? A bet is a bet."

"Yes, it is, but even though we had a deal, I'll let you off the hook. For tonight. I'll enjoy having something to hold over you."

He insisted on walking her back across the darkened lawns. A loon called on the lake and they both stopped to listen to its haunting cry.

"I don't like it that Mama was tired tonight," she said as they stood there. "She always insists on watching every movie to the end, even if it's awful. She told me once she always gives it a chance to redeem itself."

"People. Movies. She's all about second chances, our Mama. I'm concerned she's wearing herself out cooking for me. I told her to stop, but she won't."

"What rhymes with stop?" Lucy asked.

"Schnop," he said, and they shared a quiet laugh, but grew serious again as they continued walking across the backyard.

"I'm worried that it's not cooking that's wearing her out."

"Me, too."

It felt entirely too good to have someone to share these worries with.

"Has she said anything? About her health?" Lucy asked.

"No. I've been probing, too, but she says she's fine. While repairing the bathroom, I looked through the medicine cabinet. There was a prescription bottle, but she doesn't have internet, so I couldn't check what it's for."

"I can."

"I know, but it makes me feel guilty. Like I'm spying on her. It's kind of an affront to her dignity. So, I'm just going to hang out and fix the house, and keep my eyes and ears open and see if she tells me."

He stopped on her back porch.

"Good night, Lucy."

"Mac." It seemed to her suddenly she was a

long way from her goal of proving to herself that he had no power over her anymore.

In fact, it felt like everything it had always felt like with him: as if the ordinary became extraordinary, as if she'd been sleeping and was coming awake, feeling the utter glory of life shimmering through her very pores.

The moonlight and the call of the loons wrapped her in their spell.

On an impulse she stepped in close to him. She needed to know.

On an impulse she stood up on her tiptoes. She needed to know if that was the same.

She wasn't sure why she had to do this. Maybe because she felt he believed she was way too predictable, from her car to her loyalty to her little town to what he presumed was the lack of fun in her life.

She had kissed other men since then. She had something to compare him to now. She had not back then. She would not be as easy to dazzle as that girl, a virgin whose only experiences with kisses had been spin-the-bottle at parties.

Or maybe she just had something to prove to herself when she took his lips.

That she could have the power. That she didn't need to wait for other people to instigate.

But whatever her intention was, it was lost the second their lips connected. He groaned and pulled her close to him, surrendered to her and claimed her at the very same time.

Oh, no. It was the same.

It was the same way as it had always been. She had never felt it before him, and never after, either. Certainly not with the man she had nearly married.

Oh, God, had she picked James precisely because he didn't make her feel like this? No wonder he had gone elsewhere for his passion!

When Mac's lips met hers, it was as if the world melted, as if the stars began to swirl in that dark sky, faster and faster until they melted right into it and everything became one. The stars, the sky, the loons, the lake, her, Mac.

All one incredible, swirling energy that was life itself.

How was it possible that she had convinced herself she could live without this?

She could feel the danger of being sucked right into the vortex of all that energy. She could feel the danger of wanting to be sucked into it.

Instead, she forced herself to yank away.

"Damn it all to hell," she said.

"Whoa. Not the normal reaction when a woman kisses me."

Was that often? Of course it was! Look at the man!

"You stud muffin, you," she said to hide how rattled she was.

"I have the feeling if we were on the dock, I'd be getting shoved in again. Why are you so angry with me, Lucy Lin?"

"I'm not!" she said.

And she wasn't. That was the whole problem.

She wasn't angry with him at all. She loved it that he was making her laugh, and making ordinary things seem fun, and carrying the burden of Mama with her.

She loved the taste of his lips and the way his arms closed around her. It felt like a homecoming for one who had wandered too long in foreign lands.

She loved the way women looked at him in the grocery store, confirming what she always knew: Mac Hudson was about the most handsome man ever born.

And she hated herself for loving all those things.

She was angry with herself because she hadn't proved what she wanted at all. In fact, the exact opposite was true!

She had proved her life was empty and passionless, despite all her good causes!

She went in her house and closed the door, and forced herself not to look back to see him crossing the lawn in the moonlight.

"Stay on your own side of the fence!" she ordered herself grimly.

* * *

When Mac got back in, Mama was up, watching the end of the movie.

"I thought you were tired," he said.

"*Ach,* at my age, being tired doesn't mean you get to sleep. I thought the movie might redeem itself."

"Has it?"

"No. Why is this funny, people treating each other so badly?"

"I don't know, Mama." He sat down beside her, and she turned off the movie.

"What's wrong, *schatz?*"

"Mama, have I ever told you that I love you?"

"Of course," she said, with no hesitation. "Just not with words. You take time from your busy work and come to help me. What is that, if not love?"

"Too bad all women aren't as wise as you."

"When you look like me, you develop wisdom."

"I think you're beautiful," he said.

"See? What is that, if not love?"

"I'm worried about you, Mama. Living here

by yourself. The house getting to be too much for you. I'm worried you're sick and not telling anyone."

"This is a good thing, my boy. To worry about someone else, hmm? It means you are not thinking of yourself all the time."

It was hard to be offended when it was true. He lived a hedonistic lifestyle. Self-indulgent. His business had allowed him to travel the world. Collect every toy. Seek increasing levels of adventure to fill himself, for a while. His lack of commitment made him responsible to no one but himself.

When he started feeling vaguely empty, he raced to the next rush, hoping it would be the thing that would fill him.

"When you feel pain, you have to do something for another."

"I can build you a new house."

"Would that make *you* feel better?"

"Wouldn't you like it?"

"I consider having more than what I need a form of stealing."

Hmm. Hadn't Lucy said something almost the same? About his vehicles. Taking more than his share of the world's resources?

"Everybody filling up their lives full, full, full with stuff," Mama said. "What is it they don't want to feel?"

"Lonely, I guess," he surprised himself by saying. "Less than."

"Do something for someone else."

"I am. I'm doing something for you."

"You should do something nice for Lucy."

Wasn't that what he'd already decided? But now, that kiss changed everything. He felt as if he was floundering.

"She seems angry at me."

"So, that stops you? You can only offer kindness if there is something in it for you? Why is she angry at you?"

"I don't know. I mean, you know we had a little thing that summer before I left. I knew she couldn't come with me. She loved it here. The little bit of time that she was with me put her at odds with her friends and family. Her dad threatened to have me arrested he was so put out by the whole thing. We were both stupidly young. How could that have worked?"

Mama was silent, and then she said, "You left her to the only life she'd ever known. Maybe that was love, also, hmm, *schatz?*"

He was suddenly nearly blinded with a memory of how it had felt being with Lucy. Waking up with a smile on his face, needing to be with her. Practically on fire with the sensation of being alive.

He shook it off and sighed. "I'm not sure I'm capable of such nobility," he said. "She wanted more of me than I could give her."

"Ah."

"Maybe," he said hopefully, "it's not me that she's angry with. Her recent fiancé took a pretty good run at her self-esteem by the sounds of it. And something is going on with her old crowd.

I hate it that Claudia Stupid-Johnson feels better than her."

"No," Mama said softly. "What you hate is that Lucy lets her."

He felt like he was getting a headache. This was all way too deep and complicated for a guy as dedicated to the rush as he was. But while he was tackling the hard stuff, there was no sense stopping halfway.

"You didn't answer me, Mama. Are you sick?" He hesitated, and said softly, feeling the anguish of it, "Are you going to die?"

"Yes, *schatz,* sooner or later. We are all dying. From the very minute we are born, we are marching toward the other end. Why does everybody act surprised when it comes? Why does everyone waste so much time, as if time is endless, when it is the most finite of all things?"

"I don't know," he said.

"Do something nice for Lucy. It will make you feel better. And send a card to your mother."

Mama patted his cheek, got up and went up the stairs.

Well, since he wasn't sending a card to his mother, that left doing something nice for Lucy. And he knew exactly what that was. She'd somehow lost sight of who she was. She was uncomfortable going to the yacht club! Hell, she should walk in there like the queen that she was!

He thought about her lips on his.

And wondered if Mama had any idea how complicated things could get.

CHAPTER SEVEN

LUCY WAS SITTING on her deck with her laptop.
Her mother had sent her an email from Africa
with a picture attached. Her mother looked happy.
Her hair wasn't done, and she had a sunburn. It
was odd, because Lucy didn't really recall her
mother not having her hair done. And she was not
what she would have ever called a happy person.

Her inbox had more RSVPs, two more from
her old high-school crowd, saying no, they would
not be able to attend the gala.

It didn't have quite the sting it had had previ-
ously. Of course, it was a beautiful mild spring
day, the sun on the lake and her skin and in her
hair. How could you feel bad on a day like this?

Was there a possibility she was able to dismiss

negative things more easily and feel beautiful things more intensely since that kiss?

"Of course I'm not!" It was days ago! She hadn't, thank goodness, seen Mac since.

But think of the devil, and he will appear!

"Hey, Lucy Lin!" Mac was on the other side of her deck, peering through the slats of the deck railing at her. "Are you talking to yourself?"

Which would seem pathetic. Thankfully, she was not in her pajamas. It felt as if she was experiencing his sudden appearance intensely, too.

Her heart began to beat a little faster, her cheeks felt suddenly flushed. She was so aware of how incredibly handsome he was. And sexy. She was a little too aware of how his lips tasted.

He didn't wait for an answer.

"It doesn't look like you've made much progress on that paint."

"I'm not sure about the color anymore," she admitted a bit grumpily.

"Come and see what I found in Mama's shed."

She needed to pretend he wasn't there, go in

her house and follow his suggestion of locking her doors.

But, of course, if she reacted like that, he would *know* he was affecting her way too deeply.

She set her laptop aside, got up and reluctantly padded over and looked over the railing, bracing herself. With Mac it could be anything, from a snake to an antique washboard.

He grinned up at her, and she knew that was what she really needed to brace herself against.

That, and the fact Mac was holding the handlebars of a bicycle built for two. It might have been gold once, now it was mostly rust. The leather seats were cracked.

"If you promise to keep your lips off of me, I'll take you for a ride."

"Look, let's get something straight. I didn't kiss you because I find you in any way attractive."

"Hey! That was just plain mean."

"Not that you aren't." Oh! This was going sideways. "I kissed you as a way of saying thank you for caring so deeply about Mama."

"Well, I'm glad you cleared that up. Let's go for a ride."

She looked at him. She looked at the bike. She had cleared up the lip thing. Well, she hadn't really, but he had accepted her explanation. It was a beautiful day. An unexpected gift was being offered to her.

You are giving in to temptation, she told herself. "No," she told Mac.

"Look, princess, it's a bike ride or the Rollie-pop. You owe me."

Her lips twitched. Once, for a few weeks, it had felt as if Macintyre Hudson was her best friend. She could tell him anything, be totally herself around him. In many ways, it felt as if she had found out what that meant—to be totally herself—around him.

She was aware of missing that.

Could they be friends? Without the complication of becoming lovers? What would it hurt to find out?

"You're even dressed for it," he said, sensing

her weakening. "Aren't those things called pedal pushers?"

Those *things* were a pair of eighty-dollar trousers she had ordered well before her self-imposed austerity program. "It said capris when I ordered them online."

"Ah, well, you know, one born every minute."

And even though she had practiced saying no to him over and over again in her mind, she might as well not have practiced at all.

Because he was in possession of a bicycle built for two, and she wasn't in the mood to eat a Rolliepop. Plus, she was wearing an eighty-dollar pair of pedal pushers. It seemed like it would be something of a waste not to try them out!

She came down off her deck, and they pushed the bike, which was amazingly heavy, up her steep driveway to the relative flatness of Lakeshore Drive above it.

"Hop on." He took the front.

She folded her arms over her chest. "Why would you automatically get the front?"

"I assumed it would be harder."

"I think you want control. That's where the brakes are. And the steering."

"Maybe *you* want control!"

"Maybe I do," she admitted.

He sighed as if she was really trying his patience. "If you want the front, you can have it. Look, you even have the bell." He rang a rusty old bell.

He surrendered the front, and she got on the bike. He got on the back. After a few false starts, they were off.

It felt as if she was pulling him. It was really the most awful experience. Because even though his handlebars were stationary and didn't move, he acted as if they did, and every time he wrenched on them the whole bicycle shook precariously.

"Quit trying to steer!"

"I can't help myself."

"Are you pedaling?" she gasped.

"With all my might. Ring the bell and wave, we're going by your neighbor gardening."

She giggled, rang the bell and waved. The bike veered, and he tried to correct it with his handlebars that didn't work. He nearly threw them both off the bicycle. Mrs. Feldman looked up, startled, and then smiled, unaware of the problems they were having, and waved back.

They rode by the houses with name plaques at the tops of the driveways. Her father had disapproved of naming the lake properties, saying he found it corny. But Lucy liked the names, ranging from whimsical: Bide Awhile, Pair-a-Dice, Casa Costallota, to the imposing: The Cliff House, Eagle's Rest, Thunder Mountain Manor. Sometimes you could catch a glimpse of the house from the road, other times lawns, gardens, trees, lake, the odd tennis court or swimming pool.

Had she been asked, Lucy would have said Lakeshore Drive was perfectly flat. Now, it was obvious that from her house toward town, it sloped substantially upward.

She was gasping for air. "Don't run over my tongue."

"Ready to trade places?"

She did, gladly.

Though the back position was slightly more re-laxing than the front, the feeling of being out of control was terrible. She had to trust him.

"Hey, you got the easy part," she complained. The road that had been sloping upward crested, and began a gradual incline down.

"Woo-hoo! Look, no hands!"

"Put your hands back down."

"No, you put yours up. Come on, Lucy, fly!"

And so she did, and found herself shrieking with laughter as they catapulted down the hill, arms widespread, chins lifted.

His hands went back to the handlebars and so did hers.

"I think we need to slow down," she said. They were approaching the bottom of the rise, the road banked sharply to the right.

"You think I'm not trying?"

In horror, she leaned by him to see he was

squeezing the handbrakes with all his might. Nothing was happening.

"Try pushing backwards on the pedals."

He did. She did. The bike did not slow. They were coming up to the last curve into Lindstrom Beach.

He put his feet down to slow them. She was afraid he would break his leg. What his feet did was alter the course of the bike. It veered sharply left as the road went right. Her yanking away on her handlebars did nothing for their perilous balance.

They flew off the road and into a patch of thick bracken fern. She flew over her handlebars into him, and together they tumbled through the ferns. She landed on top of him, and the bike landed on top of her.

He reached up, and with one hand tenderly cupped the side of her face.

"Are you okay, Lucy Lin?" he asked with such gentleness it made her ache.

"I am," she heard herself saying. "I am okay.

I haven't been for a long, long time, but I am right now."

"That's good. That's perfect. Did I mention where we were going before we were so rudely interrupted?" Mac asked her.

"I didn't think we were going anywhere. For a bike ride."

He reached around and shoved the bike off them. She sat up, then got up. The capris were probably ruined, a dark oily-looking smudge across the front leg, a grass stain on the other side.

"Ah, actually, no. We were going to cocktail hour at the yacht club."

She glanced at him, realized he must be kidding. "You have to *dress,*" she reminded him, joking.

He was picking up the bike, inspecting it for damage. "We are dressed."

"That's not what she meant."

"Claudia had her opportunity to clarify and

she didn't. So, we're dressed or we're naked. You pick."

She suddenly saw he was serious.

"I'm not going. I've scraped my knee. I think there are leaves in my hair."

He wheeled the bike over, picked the leaves out of her hair, bent down and inspected her knee. Then he kissed it.

"You're going," he said.

"There are smudges on the front of my pants."

"Well, there's one on your derriere, too."

"I am not going to the yacht club all disheveled and smudged, with leaves in my hair! What would they think of me?"

"Why do you care what they think of you?" he asked softly.

"I wish I didn't care, but I do, okay? So far, not one of them is coming to the Mother's Day Gala."

"Why not?"

"No one in this set has ever liked Mama. My father set the tone for that years ago. They're all for doing good on paper, but they don't do it in their backyard."

"That makes me all the more committed to attending their little cocktail hour."

"Not me," she said with a shiver.

"We are going," he said, firmly. "And you're walking into that room like a queen. Do you understand me?"

She looked at him. He wasn't kidding.

"I don't want to go."

"Life's about doing lots of things you don't want to do. You're going."

And suddenly Lucy knew, with him beside her, she could do just what he had said. She could go. And she could hold her head high, too.

Suddenly, she knew he was absolutely right. She *had* to go.

She sighed. "I love it when you're masterful."

"Really? I'll have to try that more often. Back on the bike, wench."

And just like that she was riding toward what

she had feared the most for a long, long time. Only, she didn't feel at all afraid.

They rode up on their now quite wobbly bicycle built for two. She would have left it at the back door, but Mac was in the control position, and he rode along the pathway that twisted to the front of the club, where it faced the lake. Some of the cocktail crowd were out on the deck.

There was a notable pause in the conversation as they parked the bike.

Mac threw his arm over her shoulder as they went up the steps, and she glanced at his face.

He had that smile on.

If you didn't know him, you might be charmed by it.

She said quiet hellos to people on the deck, sucked in her breath and, with Mac at her side, entered the yacht club.

"Macintyre Hudson!" Claudia squealed, just in case anyone hadn't recognized him, "I'm so glad you came. Look, folks—" she looped her arm through his "—Mac is back!"

If he cared that he was in shorts when every other man was in a sports jacket and slacks, you couldn't tell.

As always, he carried himself like a king.

And she took her cue from him. Claudia was pointedly ignoring her, so she pointedly ignored Claudia.

"Ellen!" she said, finding a familiar face, "I haven't seen you for ages. What's this I hear that you don't like my paint color on my house?"

"Don't you, Ellen?" Her husband, Norman, turned and looked at her. "I like it."

Claudia's mouth puckered and pointed down. "Let me get you a drink, Mac."

"I'll have lemonade. Lucy?"

"The same."

She grinned at Mac. He had Claudia fetching her a drink!

He winked at her.

And suddenly, in this crowd of people who had once been her friends, she felt lighthearted. Had she bumped her head on the bike?

Because all these people *had* once been her friends. The girls she had known and chummed with since kindergarten. They had stopped calling her. Looked the other way when she came into a room.

And suddenly, she really didn't care. Wasn't that more about them than her? Why hadn't she picked up the phone? When had she forgotten who she was?

They all seemed so stuffy! The atmosphere in this room seemed subdued and stifling. Mac's question came back to her. *What do you do for fun?*

"Why are we all inside?" Lucy asked. "It's a gorgeous day. And Mac and I brought a bicycle built for two!"

People were looking at her! Good!

"Anyone want to try the bike?" she asked.

Silence. It was obvious no one here was dressed for this. But even so, how could they be so young and still so set in their ways? Where were their kids, for heaven's sake? Didn't they like being with their kids? That made her feel almost sorry for them.

Lucy felt determination bubbling up in her. Not to change who they were. No, not that at all. But not to hide who she was, either. Not anymore.

"There will be a prize," she said, "It's trickier than it looks!"

Still, silence. They were going to reject her. She didn't care! She was stunned by the freedom of not caring!

"The prize is complimentary tickets to the Mother's Day Gala. I have a few left."

Some of them looked uncomfortable then!

"I might throw in a free canoe rental for an afternoon. Much more romantic than those power boats tied up at the dock. That's if I'm still in business."

She was throwing their snubs back in their faces, and loving it.

"Don't pass up on this! Mac is going to serenade you with that famous song about a bicycle built for two while you ride."

She was aware of Mac giving her a sidelong look, but also of a little smile tickling the edges of his mouth that was quite different from his devil-may-care smile.

"Well, that I can't resist!" And then quiet little Beth Adams, whom she had always liked, stepped forward. "I'll try it." She gave Lucy a quick, hard hug, and said quietly, "It is so good to see you."

It was so sincere that Lucy felt tears sting her eyes.

After that it was as if a dam had burst. People coming and hugging her, shaking Mac's hand, saying how good it was to see them both.

The party moved out onto the lawn as everyone lined up to watch Beth try the bike. Beth hitched up her skirt and kicked off her shoes. Lucy got on the backseat. There was laughter and encouragement as they wobbled down the path.

"Sing," Lucy ordered Mac.

He was a good sport.

"Ring the bell," Lucy called as they turned

around at the parking lot and came back, the assembled crowd scattering off the walkway. "Don't get going too fast, the brakes are faulty."

Beth rang the bell, as Mac sang.

The way his eyes rested on her, it almost felt as if he was singing to her. He looked so proud of her!

Then Beth called her sister, Prue, to try it with her. Prue gamely hitched up her dress and tossed her shoes on the grass.

Mac started the song all over. Lucy sang with him.

And then to her amazement, everyone was singing.

Laughter flowed as others tried the bike, first some of the women together, and then couples.

It seemed everyone had to have a turn.

Mac nursed his lemonade, delivered to him and Lucy on the lawn by a very sulky Claudia. He was glad to be out of the clubhouse and back into the sunshine.

The yacht club had surprised him. Once, it had seemed like *the* place that meant you'd arrived, the exclusive enclave of the old and wealthy Lindstrom Beach families. He'd never been invited here when he lived here, nor had he attended the functions that had been open to the public, a kind of reverse snub.

Now, all these years later he'd been to places that were truly exclusive. Many of them.

And in comparison the Lindstrom Beach Yacht Club seemed like a three trying to be a nine. It had a "clubhouse" feel to it, but not in a good way. There was carpet, which was always a bad idea in a place close to water. The paneling was too dark and the paintings too somber.

He smiled as Lucy got everyone moving to the deck and then down on the lawn.

There was quite a gathering of people he'd gone to school with, some of them relatively unchanged, some changed for the worse. Most had arrived in the powerboats that were tied to the dock, and most of the women, at least, were

202 SECOND CHANCE WITH THE REBEL

"dressed," their opportunity to haul out the expensive cocktail dresses they normally wouldn't get a chance to wear.

Billy Johnson had aged poorly and had a tortured comb-over hairdo, and a potbelly.

Lucy was as he remembered her, finally. At the heart of it all. Encouraging them to laugh and have fun. Just as in the old days, they thought they were so cool, but they were chirping along to that hokey old song.

In her smudged pants and sleeveless top, with her knee bashed up, he thought she did look like queen.

He loved how she was getting everyone on that bicycle.

He loved how they were all singing that song, Lucy waving her arms around like a bandleader.

He noticed Claudia simmering beside him.

"You and Billy should try it," he said.

"Why would I?" she snapped.

"Come on, Claudia," Billy said. "Everybody but us has tried it. We could win the prize!"

She had been getting drinks when Lucy had announced the prize so Mac had to bite back a shout of laughter.

Annoyed, Claudia nonetheless did not want to seem like the only spoilsport on the lawn.

And Billy still had a bit of the captain of the football team in him. Or a few too many drinks. Because where everyone else had gone up the path and around the parking lot a few times, Billy began to go up the long steep driveway that people used to get their boats into the water.

At the top, he and Claudia disappeared onto Lakeshore Drive.

"Riding to town," someone guessed.

"Had a wreck," someone else said. "Impaired driving!"

"Oh, here they come!"

They had just turned around somewhere on the road. Claudia had obviously missed the part about the brakes, Billy had possibly already had too many drinks to get it.

As they whirred down the hill on the ancient bicycle, the little crowd burst into song.

The bike was wobbling but picking up speed. Billy was yelling, happily, "Faster! Faster!" He put his head down, pedaled with fury.

Claudia, her cocktail dress flying in the wind behind her was shrieking to him to slow down.

The crowd sang boisterously, saluting the couple with their wineglasses.

The bike careened down the hill and past the crowd. It went down the cement ramp that allowed boats to be backed gently into the lake.

Mac wasn't sure that Billy even tried the brake.

In fact, he seemed to be yelling "Ta-da" as they entered the water in a great spray of foam.

Claudia, on the backseat, flew off and into him, just as he and Lucy had done earlier.

It was spectacular! They both plunged into the water with a great splash.

Claudia floundered and squealed until Billy picked her up and hauled her out of the water. People swarmed around them. Claudia's dress looked as if it was made out of soggy toilet paper. Her hair hung in horrible ropes. Her makeup was running.

Her husband whirled her around. "Now, honey, *that* was fun! Hey, Lucy, did we win the prize?"

"Oh, you sure did," Lucy said. She was doubled over with laughter.

"What prize?" Claudia sputtered.

Mac could not take his eyes from Lucy. This is what he remembered. At the very center of it all. Only, there was something about it that was even better.

Because before, there had been no shadows in her.

And now that there were, it was twice as gratifying to see them go away. And now that there were, it was like seeing the sun after weeks of rain.

Beautiful.

The most beautiful thing he had ever seen.

CHAPTER EIGHT

"I've got to make some changes to the gala," Lucy panted. She was on the front of the bike, pedaling with all her might. They had left the yacht club and were on the final hill before her house. "I had it all wrong. It was like, when I was planning it, I was trying to win their approval. And none of them were even coming!"

"Well, they're all coming now," he said.

"That remains to be seen. They could all come to their senses before then."

"I think they just did come to their senses."

"I don't want it to be stuffy."

"Like cocktail hour was before you arrived?"

"Exactly. We need something more fun for the gala. I mean, still a dinner, and obviously it's too late to change the black-tie part, but what would you think of a comedian?"

"Lucy, please be quiet and pedal the bike!" She didn't even seem to be tired, bursting with a new energy. Mac wondered what the heck he had unleashed.

Since they knew the bike had no brakes, they walked the final decline in the road. Now that he had seen her light flicker back on, Mac felt honor bound to fan it to life, to keep it going, and it didn't take much.

Over the next few days, he did simple things. He brought a pack of hot dogs and some sticks to her place, and they roasted wieners over an open fire. And then cooked marshmallows, and ate them until their hands and faces were sticky.

He had the bike fixed and they rode it into town for ice cream.

He had one of his double kayaks sent up, and they began to explore the lake in the afternoons.

All this wholesome fun was great, but he wanted to show her more. He wanted to show her a bigger world than Lindstrom Beach. He wanted to show her he was more than the boy he had once been. That he had succeeded in a different place and moved in that place with comfort and confidence.

It occurred to him that his need to show her something more of himself was not strictly within the goal he had set for himself of showing Lucy some fun.

But since he already knew just how he would do it, he refused to ask the question whether he was going deeper than he had ever intended to go.

"Miss Lindstrom?" a deep voice, faintly muffled voice said.

"Yes?" Lucy shook herself awake, played along. She was still in bed. She looked at the clock. It was 6:00 a.m. A girl could live to wake up to the sound of his voice, even when he was trying to disguise it.

"You have won an all-expense-paid trip to Vancouver, B.C. Your flight is departing from the Freda dock in ten minutes."

That sounded so fun. And exciting. Lucy marveled at this woman she had become. But maybe they'd better set some limits.

"Mac!"

His voice became normal. "How did you guess?"

"You're the only one I know with a plane tied up at Mama's dock. I can't come—for goodness' sake, the gala is days away. This is no time to be taking off."

"Literally, taking off."

"Ha-ha."

"I'm coming over."

Something in her sighed. Mac coming over, them passing back and forth between houses as if it was the most natural thing in the world.

The truth was she couldn't wait to see him. Seeing him for the first time in a day always felt so wonderful. She told herself she had to stop this. She told herself she was playing with fire.

But she had set it off, all those days ago when he had shown up with the bicycle to see if they could be friends.

And it seemed as if they could.

Okay, so she yearned to taste him. To hold him. To kiss him. But no, that had ruined everything last time.

This time she was going to be satisfied with friendship.

She wrapped her housecoat around her and went to the door. Mac looked incredible, of course, in a nice shirt and khakis.

"You spend an awful lot of time in that housecoat, Lucy Lin."

"It's six in the morning."

He grinned wickedly. "So, what do you say? You want to come play?"

"One of us has to be a responsible adult! The gala—"

"Part of the reason for the trip," he said with sincerity.

She folded her hands over her chest, waiting to see how he was going to pull this off.

"Mama found out it's not just about Mother's Day. That it's in her honor. She's quite impressed that something at the yacht club is being held in her honor. She considers it *swanky.*"

"But it's supposed to be a surprise!"

"Come on. There are no secrets in Lindstrom Beach."

That, Lucy knew firsthand. "Did you tell her?"

He looked hurt. "No. Agnes Butterfield. It slipped out, apparently. Mama thinks it's a good thing she found out, because, according to her, she has nothing suitable to wear to such a *swanky* venue."

"Could you quit saying *swanky* like that? As if we're a bunch of small town hicks putting on airs?"

"Consider swanky banned from my vocabulary. If you'll come."

Really? A fly-in shopping trip to the big city? How on earth could she refuse that? Apparently he still thought she was resisting, and it was fun to make him try and convince her to do something she'd already decided she wanted to do.

"Mama says a galoot-head like myself cannot be trusted to help her pick a dress."

He was pushing all the right buttons. "Mac, she has more dresses and matching hats than the queen." But she said it weakly.

The carefree look melted from his face. He turned from her and looked over the inky darkness of the lake. His voice was low when he spoke. "She told me nothing she owns fits, that she lost a lot of weight last winter."

Lucy felt that ripple of fear. "I never noticed that," she said, biting a nail.

"I didn't, either. I thought it was because I hadn't seen her for a while. She said it's because she walks more, now that she doesn't have a driver's license."

Lucy closed her eyes, tried to swallow the fear and think rationally. She realized she was really dealing with two kinds of fear.

One, that something was wrong with Mama that had her losing weight and planning her own funeral.

And two, that Mac Hudson was standing on her back deck, and he still made her feel as though she was melting.

There was something quintessentially sexy about a man who could fly an airplane.

As if he knew she had given in, he said, "I told her I'd get her a new dress for her birthday. Lucy, we'll leave in a few minutes, shop, have a nice private birthday lunch with Mama and be home by early evening. It will be fun."

Oh, more fun. Didn't it seem like she was setting herself up for a heartbreak? Because he would leave and all the fun she was becoming so accustomed to would stop.

It was only a heartbreak if there was love involved she told herself. They were just friends. Besides, when was the last time she had just had a lighthearted shopping trip?

Come to think of it, Lucy realized, she was going to need a dress, too.

And come to think of it, she needed a dress that would show Mac she was not quite the stick-in-the-mud, fun-free creature he seemed to believe she was.

And maybe that she had come to believe she was, too!

Besides, wouldn't it be the best of exercises to prove that not only was she capable of embracing a spontaneous day of pure fun, but that she didn't have anything to fear from her reactions to Mac anymore?

She was a grown-up. So was he.

They could be friends. They had been proving that all week, with their strongest bond being their mutual caring for Mama Freda.

Still, this felt different than hanging out over a bonfire, eating marshmallows until they were sticky and sick.

Lucy found herself choosing what to wear very carefully. Finally, she settled on jeans, high heels, a white tailored shirt and a leather jacket. She'd finished with a dusting of makeup, a few curls in her too-short hair, and big gold hoop earrings. The look she was hoping for was casual but stunning.

And from the almost surprised male appreciation in his eyes, she had achieved it.

Mac helped Mama into the plane. Then it was her turn, and his hand closed around hers to hand her up. Given that the plane was bobbing on water, and they were stepping from the dock, this took more physical contact than Lucy had prepared herself for, but at least she didn't end up with his hand on her backside!

Her reaction to it, she told herself, was only evidence that it was time for her to stop being such a hermit.

Mama insisted on sitting in the back.

Apparently she was terrified of flying, a small detail that she was not going to allow to get in the way of a shopping trip and a new dress.

Mac leaned into the back to help her with her

seat belt, but she refused the headset Mac passed to her. Instead, out of a gargantuan red handbag, she pulled a bulky eight-track tape player. After checking batteries, she plugged in an eight-track cassette. Then, she fished through the enormous purse, pulled out a book of word searches and a pencil and hunkered down in her seat.

"Mama, there's nothing to be worried about," Mac told her.

"Worried, schmurried," she muttered without looking up from the book.

He shrugged and grinned at Lucy, then helped her buckle in, and adjusted her headset for her. There was something entirely too sexy about Mac at the controls of the plane. He was confident and professional, on a two-way radio filing a flight plan, going through a series of checks.

As the plane taxied along the lake, Lucy looked over her shoulder to see Mama jacking up the volume of her eight track and squinting furiously at her book.

"Is that Engelbert Humperdinck?" Mac asked.

"I'm sure that's what she's listening to." Lucy confirmed.

She thought she heard a sound from Mama, but when she turned around again it was to see Mama glance out the window at the lakeshore rushing by them, go pale and jack up the volume yet again.

The plane wrested itself from gravity, left water and found air. Lucy found herself holding her breath as the plane lifted over the trees at the far end of the lake and then banked sharply.

"Have you ever been in a small plane before?"

"No."

"Nervous?"

Lucy contemplated that. "No," she decided. "It's exhilarating."

Mac flew back over her house and she knew he had done that just for her. Her house from the air was so cute, like a little dollhouse, all the canoes lined up like toys on her dock.

She thought it looked very nice in white.

"Is the lavender going to be a mistake?" she said into the headset. Then, "No! No, it isn't!"

He smiled at her as if she had passed a test—not that devil-may-care smile that held people at a distance. But a real smile, so genuine she could feel tears smart behind her eyes.

She turned and tried to get Mama's attention so she could see her own house from the air, but Mama was muttering along to her music, licking her pencil furiously, and scowling at her word-puzzle book, determined not to look out that window.

"What's Caleb's House?" Mac asked.

She went from feeling safe and happy to feeling as if she was on very treacherous ground. Lucy felt her heart race. "What? Why do you ask?"

"That's the charity Mama told me she wants the money from the fund-raiser to go to. I'd never heard of it. She said to ask you."

She was aware she could tell him now. That there was something about hearing him say

Caleb's name that made her want to be free of carrying it all by herself.

But the time was not right, and it might never be right. He was here only temporarily. Why share the deepest part of her life with him? Why act as though she could trust him with that part of herself?

She had trusted him way too much once before. She had talked and talked until she had no secrets left. Now, she had a secret.

After he had left here, seven years ago, Lucy had found out she was pregnant. Terrified, she had confided in one friend.

Claudia.

Claudia had felt a need to tell her mother and father, who had told Lucy's mother and father, and maybe a few other members of their church, as well.

Lucy's decent, upstanding family had been beyond dismayed.

"How could you do this to us?" her mother

had whispered. "I'll never be able to hold up my head again."

Her father's disgust had been visited on her in icy silence. Her plans for college had gone up in smoke. Her friends had abandoned her. She had been terrified and alone, an outcast in her own town.

She had never felt so lonely.

And still, that life that grew within her had not felt like an embarrassment to her. It felt like the love she had known was not completely gone. She whispered to her baby. When she found out it was a boy, she went and bought him the most adorable pair of sneakers, and a little blue onesie.

When it had ended the way it had, in a miscarriage, it was as if everyone wanted to pretend it had never happened.

But by then she had already named him, crooned his name to him to make him feel welcome in a world where he was not really welcome to anybody but her. That was the night she had run to Mama's in her bare feet, needing to be somewhere where it would be okay to feel, to grieve, to acknowledge she could never pretend it hadn't happened.

That was the night she had spoken out loud the name of the little baby who had not survived.

Caleb.

Lucy was careful to strip her voice of all emotion when she answered.

"It's a house for young girls who are pregnant," she said. "It's still very much in the planning stages."

"One thing about Mama," he said wryly. "There's never any shortage of causes in her world."

To him it was just a cause. One of many. She took a deep breath. Was it possible he had changed as much as she had?

"Mac," she said, "tell me about you."

Part of her begged for him to see it for what it was, an invitation to go deeper.

Maybe it was different this time. If it was, would she tell him about Caleb?

"Remember I built that cedar-strip canoe?"

She nodded.

"My first sales were all those kind of canoes. It was hard to make money at it, because they were so labor-intensive, but I loved doing it. I started getting more orders than I could keep up with, so I went into production. Pretty soon, I was experimenting with kayaks, too. Two things set me apart from others. Custom paint that no one had ever seen before—canoes were always green or red or yellow, some solid, nature-inspired palette, and I started doing crazy patterns on them. It appealed to a certain market."

As much as she genuinely enjoyed hearing about the building of his business, it hardly struck her as intimate.

"The other thing was, when you bought a canoe from me, you became part of a community. I kept in touch with people, put them in touch with other people who had purchased stuff from me. Eventually, it got big enough I had to do a newsletter and a website, a social-media page and all that stuff. I didn't realize I was setting something in place that was going to be marketing gold."

Was there something a little sad about him regarding the building of relationships as marketing gold?

"They didn't just buy a canoe. They belonged to something. They were part of Wild Side. Everybody wants to belong somewhere."

"It's kind of ironic," Lucy said. "Because you seemed like you didn't have that thing about belonging." *Even to me.*

"I guess I never found anything in Lindstrom Beach I wanted to belong to."

She looked swiftly out the window.

"I didn't mean that the way it sounded."

"No, it's okay," she said stiffly. "It was just a little summer fling. I'm sure you moved on to bigger and better things. I mean, that's obvious."

"It's true I've become a successful businessman. And it's true I seem to have found my niche in life. But I've never been good at the relationship thing, Lucy. I have not improved with time. People want something I can't give them."

Was it a warning or a plea? She turned back and looked at him.

"And what is that?" she asked.

"They want to connect on a deep and meaningful level," he said, and there was that grin, devil-may-care and dashing. "And I just want to have fun."

She was not sucked in by the smile. "That sounds very lonely to me."

He raised an eyebrow. "I'm looking for someone to rescue me," he said, rather seductively, teasing.

Lucy turned back to the window and studied the panoramic views, water, earth and sky. He had always been like this. As soon as it started to go a little too deep, he turned up the wattage of that smile, kidded it away.

"Aren't you going to try and rescue me, Lucy Lin?" he prodded her.

"No," she said, and then looked back at him. "I'm going to get you a cat."

"I killed my last three houseplants."

"Wow. That takes commitment phobia to a new level. You can't even care about a plant?"

"Just saying. The cat probably isn't your best idea ever."

She sighed. "Probably not." Then she realized they were in an airplane. It wasn't as if he could jump out. She could probe his inner secrets if she wanted to.

"You always seemed kind of set apart from everyone else. It seemed like a choice, almost as if you saw through all those superficial people and scorned them."

"I don't know if *scorn* is the right word," he said. "I've always liked being by myself. I'll still choose a tent in the woods beside a lake with not another soul around over just about anything else."

"It sounds to me like someone hurt you."

His face was suddenly remote.

"It sounds to me as if you don't trust anyone but yourself."

He didn't even glance at her, suddenly intently focused on the operation of the plane, and the instrument panel.

"I'm sure my father didn't help any. I'm sorry about the way Lindstrom Beach treated you. And especially my father. When you told me how he threatened you, said he was going to set you up as a thief, I was stunned. I was more stunned that you let it work. That you let him drive you away. I always figured you for the kind of guy who would stick around and fight for what you wanted."

"And I figured you would say something to your old man in my defense, but you never did, did you?"

All these years that she had nursed her resentment against Mac, and it had never once occurred to her that she had hurt him.

"That summer," he continued quietly, "I'd never

felt like that with another person. So close. So connected. Not alone."

Lucy felt as if she couldn't breathe. It was the most Mac had ever said about how he was feeling.

"And the fact it was you, the rich girl, the doctor's daughter, loving *me*. Only, it was like you weren't the rich girl, the doctor's daughter. You stepped away from that role. You were so real, so authentic. And so was I around you. Myself. Whatever that was."

"Why didn't you at least ask me to go with you, Mac?"

"When you didn't take a stand with your dad, I guess I already knew what you would tell me later. That in the end, you would never fall for a boy like me. It would be too big a stretch for you. And unfair even to ask it."

But she was surprised by the pain, ever so briefly naked in his face. He had trusted her, and she had let him down. She could see his trust had been a most precious gift.

Lucy tried to explain. "It was only when it was obvious you were going, and you weren't going to ask me to go, that it was not even an option you had considered, that I said that. *I could never fall for a boy like you.*"

He glanced at her, searching. "It cut me to the quick, Lucy. It made me so aware of everything that was different about us when I had been living and breathing everything that was the same. I guess before you said that, I thought we'd keep in touch. That I'd phone and write. And maybe come back to visit."

Now was the time to tell him that she hadn't meant it as in he wasn't worthy of her. She had meant it as in he was too closed, he couldn't be vulnerable with her.

"Mac, I'm so sorry."

But he suddenly looked uneasy, as if he had already revealed more about himself than he wanted to, been as vulnerable as he cared to get. Some things didn't change, and she did not feel she could repair that hurt caused all those years ago by trying to clarify it now.

He must have felt the same way.

"It's all a long time ago," he said with an uncomfortable shrug. "Look where it led me. Hey, and look where we are. We're almost there. Look out your window. We'll be passing right over the Pacific Ocean in two minutes, and then making our approach to the Vancouver Flight Centre at Coal Harbour."

His face was absolutely closed. If she pursued this any farther, she was pretty sure if he had a parachute tucked behind his seat he was going to strap it on and jump.

They still had the trip home! And maybe he needed a rescuer, even as he kidded about it. She didn't know how long he was going to stick around, but she had him for today.

Maybe, just for today, neither of them needed to be lonely.

"It's only been two hours! It takes four or five

times that long to drive here from Lindstrom Beach!"

"I know. It's great, isn't it?"

"It is," she said, and suddenly felt a new willingness to let go, to embrace whatever surprises the day held for her, to embrace the fact that for some reason fate had thrown her back together with the man who had left her pregnant all those years ago. Who had hurt her.

And whom she had hurt, too. Were they being given a second chance? Could they just take it and embrace it without completely rehashing the past? Lucy found herself hoping.

"Are we landing?" Mama demanded from the back.

"Yes."

She put her puzzle book away and fished through her bag. She drew out her rosary beads.

"Hail Mary…"

Whether it was Mama's prayers or his expertise, or some combination of both they landed without incident and docked at one of the eighteen float-plane spaces at the dock.

A chauffeur-driven limousine was waiting for them, and it whisked them by the Vancouver Convention Centre to the amazing Pacific Centre Mall.

He pressed them into a very posh-looking store. The salesclerks in those kind of stores always recognized power and money, even when it came dressed as casually as Mac was.

"My two favorite ladies need to see your very best in evening wear," he said.

The clerk took it as a mission. Lucy and Mama were whisked back to private dressing rooms. Mac was settled in a leather chair and brought a coffee.

"Would you like something to read? I have a selection of newspapers."

He shook his head, but after Mama and Lucy had modeled the saleslady's first few selections, he wandered off. Lucy assumed he was restless, and didn't blame him.

Lucy had grown up with privilege, but even so, it had been Lindstrom Beach. She had never worn designer labels like these. She and Mama were in awe of how good clothes fitted, the fabric, the drape of them. Of course, even if she weren't on an austerity program, she would never be able to afford dresses like these. Even so, it was so much fun to try them on.

Mac came back, a dress over each arm. "The black for Mama, the red for you."

"Red," she said, and wrinkled her nose. "You know I'm not flashy, so you must be afraid of losing me in the parking lot. Do you have any idea what dresses like these cost?"

"The saleslady asked for my gold card before she'd even take those down for me."

"I shouldn't even try it on," she said, but heard the wistfulness in her own voice.

"You're trying it on."

"What can I say? You know I love it when you're masterful."

And so she did. She wasn't going to buy this

dress, and she certainly wasn't going to allow him to buy it for her, but why not just give herself over to the experience?

Mama went first. Lucy and Mac had "oohed" and "aahed" over the selection of designer dresses that had been brought out for Mama so far, but the one he had chosen was the best. Simple, black, silk: it was classic. Lucy and Mac applauded as Mama modeled, as if she had been on the runway all her life. She sauntered down the walkway between the change rooms, hand on her ample hip, turned, winked, flipped the matching scarf over her shoulder.

The salesclerk, Mac and Lucy applauded. Mama beamed. "This is it."

It was Lucy's turn. The clerk came into the fitting room with her to help slide the yards of red silk over her head.

Even before she looked in the mirror, Lucy could tell by the way she felt that this dress was the kind of dress a woman dreamed of.

The clerk stared at her. "That man has taste," she said.

Lucy turned and looked in the mirror. The dress had slender shoulder straps and a neckline that was a sensual V without being plunging. It had an empire waistline, tight under her breasts, and then it floated in a million pleats to the floor.

She came out of the dressing room.

"Walk like a queen," the clerk said.

That's what Mac had said, too, when he had forced her to go to the yacht club. *Walk like a queen.* In a dress like this it was easy enough to do.

When Mac saw her, his reaction was everything she could ever hope for.

She had never seen him look anything but in control, but suddenly he looked flustered.

"You," he said hoarsely, "are not a queen. Lucy Lin, you are a goddess."

She could not resist walking with swaying hips, spinning in a swirl of rich color, tossing a look over her shoulder. She licked her lips and winked.

She was trying to add a bit of levity, but Mac, for once, did not seem to find it funny.

After she had taken off the dress, Lucy came out of the dressing room, feeling oddly out of sorts. What woman tried on a dress like that and then felt okay when she walked away from it?

She went and waited outside the store while Mac bought Mama the black dress to wear at the gala.

Mama was hugging her package to her and chastising him in a mix of German and English about spending too much money on her. But they could both tell she was utterly thrilled.

They went for a fabulous lunch at a waterfront restaurant, and then, almost as if the whole thing had been a dream, they were back in the plane.

They were home before supper.

He helped her get down from the plane, then they watched Mama waddle happily across the yard with all her bags.

"Thank you for a beautiful day, Mac. It was like something out of a dream. Honestly."

He finished mooring the plane. He turned back to her.

"Okay," he said. "That's it. The whole show. I've shown you everything I do for fun. And you still haven't shown me. You said there was something."

"Oh." She felt doubtful. And then she decided to be brave. What if, by showing him, she eased that loneliness that he wore like a shield? Even for a few more hours?

"Let me make some phone calls. I'll call you in the morning."

"Phone calls to arrange fun," he said. "Sky-diving? Horseback riding? I've got it! Bungee jumping!"

"I'm afraid I'm going to be a big disappointment to you, Mac."

Or maybe to herself. Because once again, even though he had given nothing, she had made a decision to be vulnerable. She would show him that thing she did that made her feel so alive.

And he most likely wouldn't understand that there were ways a person could not feel lonely.

And how could that be anything but a good thing if he didn't understand how connected this one thing made her feel? She could have her world back the way it had been before he landed again.

Only, she had a feeling it was not going to be quite that simple.

Mac picked up the phone on the first ring in the morning.

"Are you ready for your big outing, Mr. Hudson?" Lucy asked. "Be ready in ten minutes."

"Should I be dressing for bungee jumping or horseback riding?"

"Actually, whatever you wear normally will be okay."

That could be anything from a wet suit to a suit suit, so Mac just put on some khakis and a sports shirt with the little kayak emblem on it.

He tried to take a clue from what Lucy was

wearing and came to the conclusion it would be nothing too exciting. She might have been dressed for a day clerking at the bookstore. She was not the goddess he had seen in that dress yesterday.

And wasn't that a mercy?

Still, as they got in the car, he was so aware of her. Aware he liked being with her.

"We're going to Glen Oak."

They picked up coffees and conversation flowed freely between them. They talked of Mama and house repairs, the swiftly approaching gala and last-minute details, he made her laugh by doing an impression of Claudia receiving her free tickets to the gala, which he had delivered personally.

Having spent years in Lindstrom Beach, Mac was familiar with Glen Oak. Sixty miles from Lindstrom Beach, Glen Oak was the major city that serviced all the smaller towns around it. All the large chain stores had outlets there, there was an airport, hotels, golf courses and the regional hospital.

"Golfing," he guessed. "I have to warn you, I'm not much of a golfer. Too slow for me."

"That's okay, we're not golfing."

"Not even mini?" he said a little sadly as they passed a miniature golf course. He was aware he would like to go miniature golfing with her.

And horseback riding, for that matter. He wondered what it would take to talk her into bungee jumping.

He frowned as Lucy pulled into the hospital parking lot.

"We're going to a hospital for fun?" Mac asked. "Oh, boy, Lucy, you are in worse shape than I thought."

"I tried to warn you."

Perplexed, he followed her through the main doors. She did not stop at the main desk, but the receptionist gave her a wave, as if she knew her.

What if she was sick? What if that's what she was trying to tell him? Mac felt a wave of fear engulf him, but it passed as she pushed through doors clearly marked Neonatal.

She went to an office and a middle-aged woman smiled when she saw her and came out from behind her desk and gave her a heartfelt hug.

"My very favorite cuddler!" she said.

Cuddler?

"This is Macintyre Hudson, the man I spoke to you about this morning. Mac, Janice Sandpace."

"Nice to meet you, Mr. Hudson. Come this way."

And then they were in a small anteroom. Through a window he could see what he assumed were incubators with babies in them.

"These babies," Janice explained, "are premature. Or critically ill. Occasionally we get what is known as a crack baby. We instigated a cuddling program several years ago because studies have shown if a baby has physical contact it will develop better, grow better, heal better, and have a shorter hospital stay. It also relieves stress on parents to know that even if they can't be here 24/7, and many can't because they have other children at home or work obligations, their baby is still being loved."

Lucy had already donned a gown with bright ducks all over it, and she turned for Janice to do up the back for her.

"You'll have to gown up, Mr. Macintyre."

He chose a gown from the rack. It had giraffes and lions on it. Lucy was already donning a mask and covering her hair.

Her eyes twinkled at him from above the mask.

He followed suit, as did Janice. She showed him how to give his hands a surgical scrub.

"Today we have multiples," Janice told him from behind her mask. "Twins. Preemies."

She gestured to a rocking chair. Lucy was already settled in one.

Side by side in their rocking chairs.

And then Janice brought Lucy the tiniest little bundle of life he had ever seen. Tightly swaddled in a pink blanket, the baby was placed in Lucy's arms. It stared up at her with curious, unblinking eyes.

"Amber," Janice said, smiling.

In seconds, Lucy was lost in that world. It was just the baby and her. She crooned to it. She whispered in its tiny little ear. She rocked.

This was what she did for fun.

Only, the look on her face said it wasn't just fun.

What Lucy did had gone way beyond fun. Her eyes on that baby had a light in them that was the most joyous thing he had ever seen.

Suddenly fun seemed superficial.

Lucy glanced at him. Even though she had a mask on, he could tell she was smiling. More than smiling—she was radiant.

"This is Sam," Janice said.

He looked up at her. His panic must have been evident.

"Don't worry," she said. "I'll walk you through it. Support his neck. See how Lucy is holding the baby?"

And then Mac found a baby in his arms. It

looked up at him, eyes like buttons in the tiniest wrinkled face he had ever seen.

"Talk to him," Janice suggested.

"ET, call home," he said softly. If he was not mistaken, the baby sighed. "I was just kidding. You look more like Yoda. A very handsome Yoda."

He looked over at Lucy, crooning away as if she'd been born to this.

He didn't know what to say.

And then he did.

He sang softly.

It felt as if they had been there for only seconds when Janice came back in and took the now sleeping baby from him. "Thank you," she said.

"No, thank you."

And he meant it.

They were quieter on the way home. When she drove by the mini-golf course, he didn't feel like playing anymore.

Seeing her with that baby, he had known. He had known what he had wanted his whole life and had been so afraid of never being able to have that he had pretended he didn't want it at all.

She drove into her driveway. "I have so much to get done for the gala!"

But he wasn't letting her go that easily. "Is that a charitable organization, the baby thing?" he asked Lucy.

"Yes. It's called Cuddle-Hugs."

"Why aren't we doing Mama's fund-raiser in support of that?"

"Of course they need money to operate, but that's not what Mama chose."

"I'll talk to Corporate this afternoon. I'll have them call Janice. Anything they want. Anything. They'll get it."

"That's not why I took you there, to solicit a donation."

"I know. And we didn't go to Vancouver to buy you a dress, but I bought it for you anyway."

"You bought me that dress?" she gasped.

"So, what do you think now, Lucy Lin? Could you fall for a boy like me now?"

CHAPTER NINE

IT WAS ALL wrong. It was not what he had wanted to say at all.

Mac could have kicked himself. He didn't know where the question had come from. It certainly hadn't been on his agenda to ask something like that. That certainly hadn't been the reason for his donation, the reason for the fly-in shopping trip yesterday. He hadn't done it to impress her.

It was all just a gift to her. He had found his better side after all.

But now somehow he'd gone and spoiled it all by bringing up the past. Over the past few days Mac had convinced himself that they had pretty much put the past behind them.

But really, wasn't it was always there, the past? Wasn't that why he'd made her go to the yacht club and stand up for herself? Wasn't it true that he could not look at her without seeing her younger self, without remembering the joy of her trust in him, the way she had felt in his arms, the way her heated kisses had felt scattering across his face?

She took a startled step back from him. "Oh, Mac," she said, "when I said that all those years ago, it was never about what you had or didn't have."

He gave her his most charming smile. "It wasn't? You could have fooled me."

"I guess I did fool you. Because I didn't want you to know how deeply it hurt me that you never, ever told me a single thing about you. Not one single thing about you that mattered. And then when you left, you didn't even ask me to go with you. It seems nothing has changed. Even these gifts, so wonderful and grand, are like a guard you put up. That smile you are smiling right now? That's the biggest defense of all."

"You want to know why I never asked you to go

with me, Lucy? It wasn't because I wasn't willing to fight for you. It was because you loved this place more than me. It was because I could see your family being torn up and your friends looking at you sideways as if you'd lost your mind. I gave you your life back. The part I don't get is that you didn't take it back. At all."

"No," she said, quietly, "I didn't."

"Why?"

"This isn't how it works, Mac, with you keeping everything to yourself, while I spill my guts."

"You know what? I've had about as much of Lindstrom Beach as I can handle. I wish I had never come back here."

"I wish you hadn't, either!"

He watched, stunned, as she walked away, went into her house and closed the door behind her.

With a kind of soft finality.

"Mama," he said a few minutes later, "something's come up. I have to go back to Toronto. I bought that dress for Lucy. Will you give it to her?"

"Give it to her yourself," Mama said, and went up the stairs. He heard her bedroom door slam.

Both the women he loved were mad at him.

Wait a minute! He loved Lucy? Then he was getting out of here just in the nick of time....

Lucy listened to Mac's plane take off.

"I don't care if he's gone," she told her cat. "I don't. I always knew he wasn't staying."

She had a gala to finish organizing. She had her dream of Caleb's House to hold tight to.

She burst into tears.

When the phone rang, she rushed to it. Maybe it was him. Could he phone her from the plane? Was he telling her he was turning around?

"Hello from Africa, Lucy!"

Her mother was brimming with excitement. She'd seen an elephant that day. She'd seen a lion. Somehow, Lucy didn't remember her mother like this.

"Anyway," her mother said, "I know you'll be busy on Mother's Day, so I thought I'd phone today. I didn't want you having to track me down adding an extra stress to your day."

That was unusually thoughtful for her mother. It made Lucy feel brave.

"Mom," she said, "do you mind if I paint the house purple? I mean, it's not purple, exactly, a kind of lavender."

It was kind of a segue to *Do you mind if I turn our old family home into a house for unwed mothers?*

"Lucy! I don't care what color you paint the house. It's your house!"

"Mom, did you give me this house because you felt sorry for me? Because you thought I'd never get my life together without help from you?"

"No, Lucy, not at all. I gave you that house because I hated it."

"What?"

"It was the perfect house, I was the perfect doctor's wife and you were the perfect doctor's daughter."

"Until I ruined everything," Lucy said.

"It's only in the last while that I've seen how untrue that is, Lucy. When you got pregnant, it blew a hole in the facade. When you miscarried, I thought we could patch up the hole. That everything would be the same. That you would be the same.

"But you didn't come back. You didn't want what you had always wanted anymore. I think, at first, we were all angry with you for not coming back to your old life. Me, certainly. Your friend Claudia, too.

"Now I can see how we were really all prisoners in that house. Trying to live up to your father's expectations of us. Which was a nearly impossible undertaking. Everything always had to look so good. But keeping it that way took so much energy—without my even knowing it, had sucked the life force out of me.

"That hole you blew in all our lives? I glimpsed freedom out that hole. If your dad hadn't died, I would have left him."

Lucy was stunned.

"Lucy, paint the house purple. Swim naked in the moonlight. Dream big and love hard. I'm glad you didn't marry James. He was like your father—in every way, if you get my drift. He was cold and withholding and a control freak. And he was a philanderer."

"Mom? Mac came back." Somehow this was the talk she had always dreamed of having with her mother.

"And?"

"I love him!" she wailed. "And he left again!"

"Sweetie, I can't be there. If I was I would take you on my lap and hold you and comb your hair with my fingers until you had no tears left. That's what I wish I had done all those years ago. The night the baby died."

A baby. Not a fetus. "Thanks, Mom."

"Life has a way of working out the way it's supposed to, Lucy. I am living proof of that. I love you."

"You, too, Mom. I'll be thinking of you on Mother's Day."

"Now, go eat two dishes of chocolate ice cream. Then go and skinny-dip in the lake!"

Lucy was laughing as she hung up the phone. Her mother was right. Everything would work out the way it was supposed to.

Mac was gone.

But she still had Mama, and the gala, and the babies to cuddle. Sometime, somewhere, she had become a woman who would paint her house purple, and who had a dream that was bigger than she was.

And he was part of that. Loving him was part of that.

He hadn't ruined her life. Her mother had made her so aware of that. He had given her a gift. He had broken her out of the life she might have had. He had made her see things differently and want things she had not wanted before.

That's what love did. It made people better. Even if it hurt, it was worth the pain.

Lucy was going to cry. And eat the ice cream.

She'd skip the dip in the lake. She was going to feel every bit of the glorious pain.

Because it meant she had loved. And her mother was right. Love, in the end, could only make you better. Not worse.

Mac was aware he was cutting things very close to the wire. He'd gone back to Toronto. His life had seemed empty and lonely, and no amount of adrenaline had been able to take the edge off his pain.

He loved her. He loved Lucy. He always had.

He had to give that a chance. He had to. And if it required more of him, then he had to dig deep and find that.

He was aware he was cutting things close. He arrived back in Lindstrom Beach the night before the gala.

He had never felt fear the way he felt it when he crossed back over those lawns and knocked on Lucy's door.

"Can I come in?"

When she saw it was him, Lucy looked scared to open that door. And he didn't blame her. But hope won out. She stood back from the door.

"You're in your housecoat," he said.

"It *is* nighttime." She scanned his face. "Come sit down, Mac."

The room was beautiful at night. She had a small fire burning in the hearth, and it cast its golden light across fresh tulips in a vase, a cat curled up on the rug in front of it, a book open on its spine on the arm of the chair. What would it be like to have a life like this?

Not a life of adrenaline rush after adrenaline rush, but one of quiet contentment?

A life of Lucy sharing evenings with him?

He couldn't think about that. Not until she knew the full truth. He sat on the couch, she took the chair across from him, tucked those delectable little toes up under her folded legs.

"Lucy, if you care to listen, I'm going to tell you some things I've never told anyone. Not even Mama."

Why was he doing this?

But he knew why. He could see it all starting again. She loved him. She wanted more from him. She always had.

She was leaning toward him, and he could see the hope shining in her face.

He considered himself the most fearless of men. No raging chute of white water ever put fear into his heart, only anticipation.

But wasn't this what he had always feared? Being vulnerable? Opening up to another? Tackling a foaming torrent of raging water was nothing in comparison to opening your heart. Nothing in comparison to letting someone see all of you.

But once she knew all his secrets would she still love him? Could she? Now seemed like the time to find out.

Mac took a deep breath. It was time. It was time to let it all go. It was time to tell someone. It involved the scariest thing of all. It involved trust. Trusting her.

256 SECOND CHANCE WITH THE REBEL

He hesitated, looking for a place to start. There was only one starting point.

"When I was five, my mom left my dad and me. I remember it clearly. She said, I'm looking for something. I'm looking for something *more*.

"As an adult, I can understand that. We didn't have much. My dad was a laborer on a construction crew in a small town, not so different from Lindstrom Beach. He didn't make a pile of money, and we lived pretty humbly in a tiny house. As I got older I realized it was different from my friends' houses. No dishwasher, no computer, no fancy stereo, no big-screen TV. We heated with a wood heater, the furniture was falling apart and we didn't even have curtains on the windows.

"To tell you the truth, I don't know if he couldn't afford that stuff, or if it just wasn't a priority for him. My dad loved the outdoors. Since I could walk, I was trailing him through the woods. In retrospect, I think he thought of *that* as home.

Being outside with his rifle or his fishing rod or a bucket for picking berries. And me.

"Mom left in search of something *more,* and I don't remember being traumatized by it or anything. My dad managed pretty well for a guy on his own. He got me registered for school, he kept me clean, he cooked simple meals. When I was old enough, he taught me how to help out around the place. We were a team.

"My mom called and wrote, and showed up at Christmas. She always had lots of presents and stories about her travels and adventures. She was big on saying 'I love you.' But even that young, I could tell she *hated* how my dad lived, and maybe even hated him for being content with so little.

"When she left, there was always a big screaming match about his lack of ambition and her lack of responsibility. I was overjoyed when she came, and guiltily glad when she left.

"Then she found her something *more.* Literally. She found a very, very rich man. I was eight at the time, and she came and got me and took me to Toronto for a visit with her and the new man. Walden, her husband, had a mansion in an area called the Bridle Path, also called Millionaire's Row. They had a swimming pool. She bought me a bike. There was a computer in every room. And a theater room.

"That first time I went for a visit with them, I couldn't wait to get home. But what I didn't know was that the visit there was the opening shot in a campaign.

"My mom started phoning me all the time. Every night. Why didn't I come live with them? They could give me so much *more.*

"I love you. I love you. I love you.

"What I didn't really get was how she had started undermining my dad, how she was working at convincing me only her kind of love was good. She would ask questions about him and me and how we lived, and then find flaws. She'd say, in this gentle, concerned tone, *'Little boys should not have to cook dinner.'* Or do laundry.

Or cut wood. Or she'd say, mildly shocked, '*He did what? Oh, Macintyre, if he really cared about you, you would have gotten that new computer you wanted. Didn't you say he got a new rifle?*'

"In one particularly memorable incident, I told her my dad wouldn't let me play hockey because he couldn't afford it.

"She expressed her normal shock and dismay over his priorities, and then told me she would pay for hockey. I was over the moon, and I ran and told my dad as soon as I hung up the phone.

"I can play hockey this year. My mom's going to pay for it!"

"You know, I'd hardly ever seen my dad really, really mad, but he just lost it. Throwing things around and breaking them. Screaming, 'She's never paid a dentist's bill or for school supplies, but she's going to pay for hockey? She's never coughed up a dime when you need new sneakers or a present to bring to a birthday party, but she's going to pay for hockey? What part of hockey? The fee to join the team? The equipment? The traveling? The time I have to take off work?' And then the steam just went out of him, and he sat down and put his head in his hands and said, 'Forget it. You are not playing hockey.'

"This went on for a couple of years. Her planting the seeds of discontent, literally being the Disneyland Mama while my dad was slugging it out in the trenches.

"When I was twelve, I went and spent the summer with her and Walden. I made some friends in her neighborhood. I had money in my Calvin Klein jeans. I was swimming in my own pool. She bought me a puppy. She didn't have rules like my dad did. It was kind of anything goes. She actually let me have wine with dinner, and the odd beer.

"And when summer was over, she sat down on the side of my bed and wept. She loved me so much, she couldn't bear for me to go back to *that* man. She told me I didn't have to go back. She said I didn't have to think about my dad or his feelings. I should have seen the irony in that—

that my dad's feelings counted for nothing, but hers were everything, but I didn't.

"I was twelve, nearly thirteen. At home, my dad made me work. By then, I was in charge of keeping our house supplied with firewood. I did a lot of the cooking. Sometimes he took me to work with him and handed me a shovel. I was allowed to go out with my friends only if I'd met all my obligations at home.

"And here she was offering me a life of frolic. And ease. I saw all the *stuff* I could ever want. I could be one of the rich, privileged kids at school instead of Digger Dan's son.

"I phoned my dad and told him I was staying. I could hear his heart breaking in the silence that followed. But she had convinced me that didn't matter. Only *I* mattered.

"And that's what I acted like for the next few months. Like only I mattered. She encouraged that. When my dad called, sometimes I blew him off. I was supposed to spend Christmas with him, but I didn't want to miss my best friend's New

Year's Eve party, so I begged off going to be with him."

Mac took a deep shuddering breath. "Do you remember, a long time ago, I told you I killed a man?"

"With your bare hands," she whispered.

"Not with my bare hands. With my self-centeredness. With my callousness. With my utter insensitivity.

"He died. My dad died on Christmas Day."

"Oh, Mac," she whispered.

"At home, all by himself. He managed to call for help, but by the time they got there he was gone. They said it was a massive heart attack, but I knew it wasn't. I knew I'd killed him."

"Oh, Mac."

"Killed that man who had been nothing but good to me. He might not have been big on words. I don't think I heard him say 'I love you' more than twice in my whole life. But he was the one who had been there when no one else was, who had stepped up to the plate, who had done his best to provide, who had taught me the value of hard work and honesty. I had traded everything he taught me for a superficial world, and I hated myself for it.

"And her. My mother. I hated her. When she told me she didn't see the point in me going to the funeral, that was the last straw. I ran away and went back. To his funeral, to sort through our stuff.

"I never lived with her again. I couldn't. When they tried to make me go back to her, I ran away. That's how I ended up in foster care.

"I haven't spoken to her in fourteen years. I doubt I ever will again. I can see right through her clothes and her makeup, her perfect hair and her perfect house. She plays roles. For a while I was the role and she could play at being the fun-loving, cool mom, because it filled something in her. It relieved her of any guilt she felt about leaving me when I was little.

"But underneath that veneer she was mean-spirited and manipulative, and basically the most

selfish and self-centered person ever born. She was using me to meet her needs, and I was done with her.

"I went through a series of foster homes, crazy with grief and guilt. And then I came here. To Mama Freda.

"And Mama saw the broken place in me, and didn't even try to fix it. She just loved me through it.

"I owe Mama my life."

The silence was so long. There, Lucy had it all. She knew the truth about him. He was the man who had killed his own father.

"When you told me, all those years ago, that you had killed a man, I thought you were blowing me off," Lucy whispered.

When had she moved beside him? When had her hand come to rest on his knee?

"I started to tell you. Back then. I saw the look on your face and retreated to the default defense. I always told people that when I was trying to drive them away, protect myself. I added the part about *with my bare hands* because it seemed particularly effective."

"You feel as if you killed your father," she said, looking at him. The firelight reflected off her face. In her eyes he saw the same radiance he had seen when she held the baby.

It hadn't been pity for the baby. And it wasn't pity for him.

It was love. It was the purest love he'd ever seen.

"I did kill my father," he whispered, daring her to love him anyway.

"No," she said, firmly, with almost fierce resolve. "You didn't."

Three words. So simple. *No. You. Didn't.*

Her hand came to his face, and her eyes were so intent on his.

It felt like absolution. It felt as if, by finally naming it out loud, the monster that had lived in the closet was forced to disappear when exposed to light.

He'd been a teenage boy who did what teenage boys do, so naturally. He had been selfish and thoughtless and greedy. He'd thought only of himself.

It didn't have to be who he was today. It wasn't who he was today.

"You're terrified of love," she said.

"Terrified," he whispered, and knew he had never spoken a truer word.

And she didn't try to fix him. Or convince him. She laid her head on his chest, and wrapped her arms hard around him. He felt her tears warm, soaking through his shirt, onto the skin of his breast.

Her tenderness enveloped him.

And he knew another truth.

That she would see him through it.

Mama's love had carried him so far. Now it was time to go the distance. If he was strong enough to let her. If he was strong enough to say yes to something he had said no to for the past fourteen years.

Love.

He suddenly felt so tired. So very tired. And with her arms wrapped around him, with his head on her breast, he slept, finally, the sleep of a man who did not have to go to his dreams to do battle with his guilt.

When he awoke in the morning, she was gone. The coffee was on, and there was a note.

"Sorry, three zillion things to do. The gala is tonight!"

He went back over to Mama's. Overnight the population there had exploded. Her many foster children wandered in and out, many of them with children of their own. There were tents on the lawn and inflatable mattresses on the floor.

"You stayed with Lucy?" Mama asked, in a happy frenzy of cooking.

"Not in the way you think. Mama, come outside with me for a minute." He found a spot under the trees, and took a deep breath. "Lucy asked some of your foster children to speak at the gala tonight. She chose a few. I was one of them and I've said no. But I think, with your permission,

I'll change my mind. But only if you'll allow me to share that story you told me all those years ago."

"*Ach.* For what purpose, *schatz?*"

"For the same purpose you told it to me. To let everyone know that in the end, if you hold tight, love wins."

Her eyes searched his. She nodded.

The gala was sold out. He had seen Lucy flitting around in her red dress. He had told her he would speak.

But it seemed to him strange that with the big day here, the day that she had given her heart and soul to, she seemed wan.

"Are you not feeling well?" he asked her.

"Oh," she said. "No. I'm fine. I thought my doing this…" Her voice faltered. "Mother's Day is hard on me."

"Why? Because your own mother is so far away?"

"I'm just being silly," she said. "Sorry. I think I'm a little overwhelmed."

"Everything looks incredible. The silent auction is racking up bids."

She smiled, but it still seemed wan, disconnected.

He had the awful thought it might be because of what he had shared with her last night.

"I think the custom-painted Wild Ride kayak is going to be the high earner of the night."

"It will be. I keep pushing up the bid on it."

He expected her to laugh. She ran a hand through her hair, looked distracted.

"Oh," she said brightening slightly. "He's here."

"Who?"

"I couldn't find a comedian on such short notice. I found something Mama will like even better. An Engelbert impersonator."

He waited for her to smile. But she didn't. She looked as if she was going to cry.

"Later," she said, and walked away.

After dinner, some of Mama's foster children

spoke. Ross Chillington talked about his parents being killed in an accident and about coming to Mama's house, how she was the first one who ever applauded his skill in acting.

Michael Boylston told how Mama had given him the courage and confidence to take on the world of international finance and how now he lived a life beyond his wildest dreams in Thailand.

Reed Patterson told of a drug-addicted mother and a life of pain and despair before Mama had made him believe he could take on the world and win.

And then it was his turn. But he didn't talk about himself.

"A long time ago," he said, "in a world most of us in this room had not yet been born into, there was a terrible war." And then he told Mama's story.

When he finished, the room was as silent as it had been that day fourteen years ago when he had first heard this story.

Into the silence he laid his next words with tenderness, with care.

"Mama spent the rest of her life finding that soldier. She found him over and over again. She found him in every lost boy she took into her home. She found him and she saved him. She saved him before the great evil had a chance to overcome him.

"I am one of those boys," he said quietly, proudly. "I am one of the boys who benefited from Mama's absolute belief in redemption, in second chances.

"I am one of those boys who was saved by love. Who was redeemed by it. And as a result, finally, was able to love back.

"Mama." He looked right at her. "I love you."

The words felt so good. She was weeping. As was most of the audience. His eyes sought Lucy. It wasn't hard to find her in her bright red dress. She had her face buried in her hands, crying.

Mac realized right then that he had a new mission in life. He had not killed his father. But it was possible that he had contributed to his death.

He could not change that. But he could try to redeem himself. He could spend the rest of his life on that. Make up for every wrong he had ever done by loving Lucy. And their children. By believing all that love was a light, and when it grew big enough it would envelop the darkness. Obliterate it.

Lucy still didn't look right. She was in her element, surrounded by people. She had just pulled off something incredible. But she was still crying.

And suddenly she spun around and went into the night.

He waited for her to come back, especially when the Engelbert impersonator geared up and the tables were cleared away for dancing.

Mama stood right in front of the stage. She took off her scarf and threw it at the man's feet.

He picked it up and wiped his sweaty brow, and tossed it back to Mama, who looked as if she was going to die of happiness. Michael Boylston came and asked her to dance. Mac watched and shook his head.

If Mama was unwell, there was no sign of that now. None.

It occurred to Mac that there was something of the miraculous in this evening.

Those foster kids who had grown into adults seemed to be the first to take to the floor, having embraced so much of Mama's enthusiasm and joy for life. They were asking others to dance with them, and, in some instances, were dancing with the people who had once snubbed them as the riffraff from Mama's house.

Claudia was trying to get Ross to sign a movie poster with him on it. Over in the corner, Billy was drinking too much and talking football with Reed Patterson.

Lucy had done what she always did best. She had brought people together.

It hit him out of nowhere.

Things on her dining-room table she didn't want him to see.

Rezoning that had the neighbors in an uproar.

Caleb's House: a home for unwed mothers.

Finding joy in holding little babies.

Mother's Day is hard on me.

It hit him out of nowhere: all her plans had been altered. Claudia feeling superior to her. Her friends not being her friends anymore. No college. Moving away from here. And coming back. Changed.

"Oh my God," he said out loud, and he headed for the door.

There was still, thankfully, a little light in the evening sky. If it had been darker, he might not have been able to see her.

But as it was, her red dress was like a beacon in the thick greenery above her house.

Mac went toward that beacon as if he was a sailor lost at sea. There was a trail, well-traveled along the side of her house, that led him to her.

She was in a small clearing above her house,

sitting on a small stone bench. There was a little flower bed cut from the thick growth. In the center of that bed was a stone, hand-painted in the curly cursive handwriting of a girl.

Caleb.

He went and sat beside her on the bench. "There was a baby," he said, and it was a statement not a question. His mouth had the taste of dust in it.

"They said not to name him," she choked. "They said he wasn't even a baby yet. A fetus. They wouldn't let me bury him. He was disposed of as medical waste."

She was sobbing, and he felt a grief as deep as anything he had ever felt.

"He was mine, wasn't he?"

"Yes, Mac, he was yours."

So many questions, and all of them poured out, one on top of the other. "Why didn't you tell me? Were you planning on telling me? Would you have told me if he lived?"

"Mac, I was at the scared-out-of-my-mind stage. I knew Mama would know where you were. I'd decide to tell you. I'd even cross the lawn to Mama's house. And then I'd talk myself out of it. I felt that you would come back—not for love, but because I'd trapped you into it."

"I had a right to know."

"Yes," she said softly, ever so softly, "Yes, you did. And I think, eventually, I would have finished that million-mile journey across her lawn. But then the baby was gone, and the pain was so bad that the last person I was thinking of was you."

Mac was silent. He could feel that pain unfurling in him. *His baby. His and hers.* It made life as he had lived it so far seem unreal. How would he have been different if he had known?

"When were you going to tell me?" he finally asked.

"Soon," she whispered. "I hoped to get through Mother's Day. If you hadn't come back I was going to call you. I knew it was time. To trust you with it."

He looked at her, and knew it was true. And he knew something else. That he had to rise to the fragile trust she was handing him. This had been her secret, her intensely personal grief, but it was no longer. This pain would be an unbreakable bond between them.

Something that they, and they alone, would know the full depth of.

In this instant he sat beside her and felt her grief, and he felt his own. He felt a momentary hurt that he had been excluded from one of the biggest events of his own life.

And yet looking into her eyes, he felt his hurt dissolve and he was taken by the bravery he saw in her. Her hands were clutched around something, and he unfolded them from around it.

It was a small box.

"I bring it with me when I come here."

"May I look?" His voice sounded gruff, hoarse with unshed emotion.

Lucy nodded through her tears, her eyes on his face, begging him.

Inside was a tiny pair of sneakers. A blue onesie with a striped bear embossed on it. And an ultrasound picture.

Begging him to what? To love her anyway, when everyone else had stopped? That was a given.

He touched the little sneakers to his lips. He had not wept since his father died. But he wept now, on Mother's Day, for the baby who would have been his son.

And that's when he saw what she was really begging him for. Someone to share this love with him. The love she had carried alone for too long.

He vowed to himself she would not be alone with it anymore. Not ever.

He saw so clearly what was being given to them both. A chance at redemption. A chance to make good come from bad.

A chance for love to grow from this garden where there had been sorrow.

A long time later they sat in silence, their hands intertwined. The sounds from the party below them grew more boisterous.

The sounds of "I Can't Take My Eyes Off You" floated up through the air.

"You know we would have never made it if I'd asked you to come with me all those years ago."

"I know."

"But I think we could make it now."

She turned to him, her eyes wide with love and hope.

Mac felt now what he could never have felt back then, as a callow youth. The complexity of loving someone.

"I'm asking you to marry me, Lucy Lin, I'm half crazy all for the love of you."

"Yes," she whispered, and then stronger, "Yes."

"You know, Lucy," he said, softly, his voice still gruff with emotion, "it won't all be a bicycle built for two. There are going to be hurts. And misunderstandings. I have places in me that are so tender they will bruise if you try to touch them. It's going to be a lifelong exercise in building trust."

She leaned her head on his shoulder. "I know what I'm getting into."

He watched the moonlight in her eyes and saw that the light coming from them was radiant.

"I do believe you do, Lucy Lin."

Mac took Lucy in his arms, and her soft warmth melted into him and he thanked God for second chances.

EPILOGUE

MACINTYRE HUDSON SIGHED AS a rush of girlish laughter filled the air. Mother's Day was still a whole week away, but Caleb's House, next door to this one, was filled to capacity. There were two trucks with campers on them parked up on the road. No doubt Claudia would be by shortly to complain about that.

There was no official Mother's Day celebration at Caleb's House, but they always came back, those girls, turned into young women, who had stayed there.

They came back whether they had kept their babies or given them up for adoption.

They were drawn back there as if by a spell. Every year, at the same time, they came.

Some came with families—mothers and fathers

they had reconciled with, or young husbands who had accepted their history and stepped up to the plate for their future. They came with new young babies and toddlers.

They joined whoever was in residence now, and pretty soon the giggling started and carried across the lawns of that beautiful lavender house to this one.

Mama's house was long since gone. He'd torn it down, and he and Lucy had built a new one. It had what was called a mother-in-law suite, but they moved back and forth between the two living spaces seamlessly. Mama particularly liked their kitchen with all its shiny stainless-steel appliances, even though she didn't make *apfelstrudel* very often anymore.

But it was still *her* house, and ever since the gala, so many of those children Mama had fostered came back on Mother's Day weekend. Came back to the place where they had learned the meaning of home.

Right now, this part of Lakeshore Drive looked like a carnival.

"Did you see this?" Lucy came up behind him.

The funeral-planning kit was out on the table, where they could not miss it.

"Do you know what it's about?" she asked, that cute little worry line puckering her forehead.

"She was staring out the window the other day, lamenting the fact she might not see our children before she dies."

"I guess we should tell her, hmm?" Lucy said.

"No! I don't want her thinking every time she produces that brochure we're going to have a baby for her. Aren't there enough of them next door?"

"*Ach,*" Lucy said, imitating Mama, "a baby is always a blessing."

Those words were a motto, and hung on a smaller sign right below the one that read Caleb's House.

Lucy wrapped her arms around him from behind, nestled into him for a moment and sighed with utter contentment. Then she went to the fridge and took out a jar of Rolliepops.

She popped one in her mouth.

"Those things can't be good for the baby."

"Who are you kidding? You hate kissing me after I've had one. Can't help it. Cravings." She removed a large stainless-steel bowl of potato salad.

"Potluck at Caleb's tonight," Lucy said. "Between Mama's kids and my kids, I think there must be a hundred people out there. Have you seen my mom?"

"She went through here with Donald on her hip a while ago, muttering about diapers." Donald was the baby she had brought back from Africa.

Next year there would be one more added to this amazingly diverse, huge and loving family Mac found himself a part of.

"Are you coming?" Lucy asked. "They'll be starting in a few minutes."

"Give me a minute."

Funny how even after all this time, the sound

of his son's name, the son whom had never been born and who he had never known, still squeezed at his heart.

Mac went back to the table. Beside the funeral-planning kit, Mama had set out a card.

He picked it up. On the front it said, "Happy Mother's Day." Inside was completely blank. He set it back down, then went and stood at the window and looked over the familiar sparkling waters of Sunshine Lake.

His own child would be coming into this world soon.

It would require more of him.

Love required more of him. He had thought it would be a lifetime exercise to build trust, but he had never been so wrong.

He trusted Lucy implicitly. He trusted himself to be the man she and Mama believed he was. He trusted in life. Hadn't it become joyous and sweet beyond his wildest dreams?

Mac fished through the junk drawer until he found a pen, and then he went and sat down at the old kitchen table that they could never replace. It was the *apfelstrudel* table. He stared at the card for a long time, and then opened it.

How to start?

And so he started like this.

Dear Mom,

Not too much. A few lines. That she would be a grandmother soon. That she had not met his wife yet. That maybe they could get together the next time he was down east.

He signed it, licked the envelope, addressed it and put a stamp on. Maybe, just maybe, they would have a chance to redeem themselves.

Mama waddled in and went right to the fridge. "Where's the potato salad? My German one. Not like the stuff they call potato salad here."

"Lucy took it already."

"Are you coming, my galoot-head? Listen. They're singing grace."

All those voices raised in a joyous song of

thanks. His Lucy would be at the very center of it, where she belonged.

"I'll be along in minute. I'm going to run up to the mailbox first."

Mama's eyes shot to the table, where the card had been.

Mac thought you could live for moments like this: a heart filled with love, the sound of gratitude drifting in the window and a smile like the one Mama gave him.

* * * * *

Mills & Boon® Large Print
September 2013